stray

STACEY GOLDBLATT

stray

A
NOVEL

DELACORTE PRESS

Published by Delacorte Press
an imprint of Random House Children's Books
a division of Random House, Inc.
New York

Delacorte Press and colophon are registered trademarks of
Random House, Inc.

www.randomhouse.com/teens
Educators and librarians, for a variety of teaching tools,
visit us at www.randomhouse.com/teachers

Library of Congress Cataloging-in-Publication Data
Goldblatt, Stacey.
  Stray / by Stacey Goldblatt. — 1st ed.
    p. cm.
  Summary: Natalie's mother, a veterinarian with a dogs-only practice, has
the sixteen-year-old on such a short leash that, when the teenaged son of
her old school friend comes to stay with them for the summer, Natalie is
tempted to break her mother's rules and follow her own instincts for a
change.
  ISBN: 978-0-385-73443-1 (trade) — ISBN: 978-0-385-90448-7 (glb)
  [1. Mothers and daughters—Fiction. 2. Behavior—Fiction. 3. Identity—
Fiction. 4. Dogs—Fiction. 5. Dating (Social customs)—Fiction.
6. Friendship—Fiction.] I. Title.
  PZ7.G56449St 2007
  [Fic]—dc22
                        2006031828

The text of this book is set in 12-point Baskerville.

Printed in the United States of America
10 9 8 7 6 5 4 3 2 1
First Edition

A dog that exhibits improper conduct is a social hazard. —Michael Kaplan, *The Manifesto of Dog*

Fun used to be simple.

"C'mon, Natalie," says Laney. "Show us yours!" She's bouncing on the couch with her shirt off and wine spilled down the legs of her hip-hugging pajama pants. Since fruit is the grading scale, Laney's are judged to be cantaloupes. So far, hers are the biggest.

"No, thanks," I say. I can't just merrily yank up my T-shirt in front of a group of girls who probably won't have the courtesy to wait and laugh at me behind my back. Nothing has changed between the beginning of seventh grade and tonight, the last night of our sophomore year at Portola High School, to convince me that these girls aren't like a clannish pack of Chihuahuas, who, like all creatures popular and elite, don't fancy other breeds.

Not that I'm escaping humiliation entirely. During truth or dare, I had to lick Candace Mortin's pinkie toe.

But choosing "truth" would have been worse in the long run. This is not a crowd who'd be plucking questions from the "what's your favorite color?" category. No, they'd blast right over to some million-dollar question about fornication. And although I am proud that I haven't subjected myself to some blistery sexually transmitted disease, I'm not carrying around a banner proclaiming my virginity.

The only reason I'm here in the first place is that my best friend, Nina, was invited. I shoot a glance at her. Besides me, she is the only girl fully clothed. But she's no help, screaming lyrics a cappella into a half-empty wine bottle with Maryann McClure, the hostess of this evening's debacle.

Laney interrupts Nina and Maryann's duet. "Your turn, Nina!"

With fingers still curled around the wine bottle, Nina hikes up her tank top. "Lemons!" Maryann announces.

"Not lemons," Laney says. "Those are peaches!"

"Yes!" Nina yells, pumping her fist. "Stone fruit!" She unrolls her shirt back down over her belly and dramatically points a finger at me. "Natalie, you're up." She is kidding, right?

"Yeah, Natalie. C'mon," says another girl. "You've seen ours."

Actually, I've been trying not to look. And not once have I shouted a fruit, although I do think Kelsey Pearson's are definitely bigger than kiwis. But I saw hers only because she catwalked like some runway model in my direction with her boobs aimed at eye level.

Laney swerves her hips toward me. "You haven't even had anything to drink, have you?"

I am going to have to do this. There will be prolonged laughter, because I am dressed like a hobo. My strawberries are tucked underneath three layers: a sweatshirt, my Pug Lovers Rescue T-shirt, and a bra so old it looks like it's been used in numerous games of tug-of-war.

They are starting to chant. "Nat-a-lie! Nat-a-lie! Nat-a-lie!"

Outside the sliding glass door, Maryann's basset hound starts howling. She walks over and shoves the door open. "Shut up, Bogart!" She gives him a hard slap on his snout. "Stupid dog."

Jen Wexler covers her mouth and starts running toward the bathroom. "She's gonna puke!" someone screams.

The girls flock toward her.

Taking advantage of Jen's attention-getting sprint to the toilet, I slip outside with my backpack in tow to join Bogart. The wrinkles bunched on his face slink back when he looks up at me; with his short legs, his long stocky body could be compared to a coffee table.

I bend down to offer him my palm and receive a tail-wagging response.

In a matter of minutes, Bogart and I are sitting in a wicker lounge chair on the back patio, hidden from the party inside. We gaze at the full Thursday moon in its veil of coastal fog. I stroke his long velvety ears as he rests his head on my stomach. His droopy eyes look at me as if I am his universe.

If only I could attract boys the way I attract dogs.

The night was bound to go awry because I am not a card-carrying member of this popular crowd. My being here is partly a result of Nina's down-on-her-knees begging me. But I think there was also a hint of hope that maybe, just maybe, I'd have a good time with these girls.

The truly amazing thing about all this, though, is not that I was invited. It's that Mom let me spend the night here despite her not getting the opportunity to screen and fingerprint Maryann's parents, who, contrary to what I told Mom, are not here.

When I stopped by work this afternoon, Mom called me into her office and questioned me with suspicion, pushing for a clear and accurate character sketch of Maryann. It was a must-embellish situation, so I told her Maryann was an honor student and treasurer of the Good Samaritan Society.

I'm just hoping that my mother doesn't gain access to Maryann's report card or thumb through my yearbook and discover that the young Samaritans of my high school did not band together to form a club.

Bogart's throat quivers against my leg as he lets out a snore that rivals the deep chortle of a pig: at least the night wasn't a complete waste of a lie.

I am not compulsive about lying. Having lived with the betrayal of a cheating father, I value the truth, so even though I hate that Mom is overbearing, I do feel obligated to be honest with her.

That said, to maintain a shard of a social life and prevent Mom unnecessary grief, I entitle myself to withholding or fabricating information two times per season, which gives me an allowance of eight lies per year. I have yet to meet my quota but it's nice to have the wiggle room should I need it.

And I needed to lie about Maryann. There is no benefit to Mom's knowing that Maryann got sent home from school last year for violating the dress code (how was Maryann to know that it wasn't appropriate to wear a thong under a short skirt?) and that she is the type of girl who has pet names for guys' wieners (a lovely tidbit confessed during tonight's truth or dare session). Mom is better off without this information.

Voices rise inside the house and the contest continues with an upsurge of energy. "Tomatoes are too a fruit, you dork!"

I got out of it this time, but if this is the direction of my social life, I'm going to have to stop being a walking advertisement for the rare and endangered straight-edged sixteen-year-old, even if that means filling a cup with wine and pretending to drink it.

I hate to admit it, but I might be good at pretending. It's just that no matter how hard I try to pretend, it never feels quite real.

I release a heavy sigh. Bogart licks my hand because he understands. Most dogs do.

To a dog, a crate does not represent entrapment but safety. —Michael Kaplan, *The Manifesto of Dog*

When I wake the next morning, my fingers try to untangle the web of brown hair that's hanging in front of my eyes.

The sun is locked in a tomb of clouds. Bogart conducts a search-for-food mission in my backpack. We're still in the lounge chair on the patio, but I feel like I've been shrouded in morning dew.

A mound of bras lies over my stomach, and an empty raisin box is positioned in the crook of my arm. This is devastating. I thought my chest would at least qualify for the berry category. But reality is staring me in the face: there is no unit of fruit smaller than a raisin.

I look at my watch. 6:49 a.m. Friday. Officially the

first day of summer vacation. And I need to be at work by eight o'clock this morning.

Bogart nudges underneath my chin. "You hungry, boy?" I inspect the yard and find a mold-laden water dish with about an inch of murky water in it. Besides a disappointed cockroach, there's nothing in Bogart's food bowl.

A muffled version of "Yellow Submarine" pipes from my backpack. Kirby's ringtone. I still have his phone. Yesterday after school he put it in my bag so that it wouldn't get wet while we were running through the sprinklers on the football field: a last-day-of-school tradition.

I flip open the phone. "Hello?"

Kirby's voice trails from the other end. "Where are you?"

"Maryann McClure's backyard."

"By yourself?"

"Kind of," I answer, not wanting to dismiss the presence of Bogart (who has just collapsed in exhaustion at my feet).

"Told you."

"Told me what?" I ask.

"That you'd end up having a horrible time."

"What's that got to do with me being in Maryann's backyard?"

"You're out there because those girls are oxygen-hogging alpha females. You had no choice but to retreat outside for some fresh air."

"Who are you, the host of a *National Geographic* special?"

"Nope, just a friend who tells it like it is," Kirby answers. "So, are you okay?"

"I'll live." My phone starts barking inside my backpack, the Little Angry Dogs ringtone. The realistic shrill of yipping dogs sends Bogart into a delirious bout of howling. "My phone's ringing." I hold Kirby's phone between my shoulder and ear and try to shush Bogart so that he won't wake everyone up.

"Why am I not surprised to hear a real dog barking in the background?" Kirby asks.

"Gotta put you down for a minute, Kirb, hold on." I throw his phone onto the bra-strewn chair. Fortunately Bogart's howl stifles because his nose is now sheathed in my backpack as he sniffs around for the tiny bundle of dogs he believes have come to life in there. I find my phone and answer. "Hello?"

"Good morning. Just wanted to make sure you're awake." Mom.

"I'm up." Doesn't she understand that I am capable of waking up without the alarm clock of her voice piercing my eardrums?

"Do you need me to come and get you?"

"Actually, Kirby's going to swing by and pick me up."

"Don't be late," Mom says. "Love you."

"Love you, too," I reply, but she's already hung up the phone.

"So I'm coming to get you?" Kirby asks when I pick up his phone again.

"I do have your phone. And I need some help."

"I will forgo the drop-off box in order to assist you, Nat."

"Thanks for making the sacrifice, Kirb."

Kirby's mom, Eve, owns and runs Rescued Threads, a used clothing store and one of the coolest places in all of Beacon, California. For Kirby, early-morning scavenging through the drop-off box, a huge lime-colored Dumpster, is like Charlie's search for the Golden Ticket in a Wonka candy bar. He's found many a prized possession going through the drop-off box: an old pair of cowboy chaps, a vintage Ramones Rock 'n' Roll High School T-shirt, and a vest made out of yarn and bottle caps.

Kirby and I arrange to meet at the corner in eight minutes.

Before I leave the yard, I peek through the sliding glass door. Limp girls lie passed out on the floor as if they fell where they were standing because their batteries died. Nina is curled on the couch with a sweatshirt draped over her tiny body. I am tempted to tap her on the shoulder and whisk her away. But unlike me, Nina is comfortable with those girls.

Somewhere along the timeline of my human development, I missed an important socialization period. My dad told me one time that a puppy needs to interact with at least a hundred people and a hundred dogs in the first two years of its life for it to become "socially flexible." Maybe people do, too. This may explain why I am socially stunted and on the outside of Maryann's house looking in.

Bogart follows me out the side gate. He is officially a runaway dog. There is no choice but to save him.

We wait on the curb, watching a few cars hum by, until Kirby's rusted yellow Civic hatchback arrives, whirring like a windup toy.

Bogart and I burrow into the passenger side.

Kirby's messy brown hair is trying to escape from his hooded sweatshirt. "Morning, glory." He looks at Bogart through the thick lenses of his black-rimmed glasses. "Another one? Didn't you just save a dog like a week ago?" I nod. "You're such a slut."

I return Kirby's phone to him, then fasten my seat belt. Bogart sits pouched on my lap like a baby kangaroo. I can't put him in the backseat because it was ripped out in one of the car's previous lives.

"This is Bogart, Maryann's dog."

"Nice to meet you," Kirby says to Bogart. He reaches over and shakes Bogart's chunky paw, noticing his overgrown claws. "Those are some long-ass nails you've got, buddy."

"Poor guy is being neglected, aren't you, handsome?" I rub Bogart's thick neck with my hands. He looks back at me with saggy-eyed appreciation.

"Where's Nina?" Kirby asks before shifting into gear.

11

"Sleeping on Maryann's couch and clinging to a wine bottle for dear life. It was her microphone." I tell Kirby about the wine-bottle karaoke scene as he guides the car onto the stretch of road ahead.

"Anything else?" Kirby asks.

"If you must know, I was asked to flash my hooters." The car swerves to the left, and Kirby tightens his grip on the steering wheel. Note to self: stay away from discussing boobs with Kirby. At least while he's driving.

"Well, then," he says, pushing through the awkwardness. He clears his throat. "How 'bout some tunes? Franz Ferdinand?"

"I'd love some." Kirby turns up the volume, and music thunders through the speakers. The car may be run-down, but the same cannot be said for the stereo system that is stashed away in the glove compartment.

Serenaded by Franz Ferdinand, we drive several blocks. When we turn the corner onto my street, I can barely see my two-story house at the end of the cul-de-sac. As we get closer, it looks whitewashed and bare, surrounded by a moat of yellow dandelion weeds.

Next door is Laney Benning's house, its generous porch winding around the front. I wonder if Laney's mom, Trina, Beacon's number-one-real-estate-agent-third-consecutive-year-running, can imagine her own daughter encircled by empty wine bottles or if she'll wake picturing Laney in the safety of a pink sleeping bag with a crumpled can of Coca-Cola in her hand.

Kirby points his thumb toward Laney's as he parks in front of my house. "What was she doing last night?"

"During truth or dare she shared that she made out with two different guys at Austin Keely's party."

"Fun!" He nails the sarcasm and turns off the Civic.

My mom's car is gone, so she's already at work. "I'm gonna go upstairs real quick."

"Hurry."

"Stay with him?" I ask.

Kirby looks at Bogart and groans. "It looks like his skin is sliding down his face."

"Watch it. You're looking at a breed that's the second-best sniffer of all dogs. All dogs, Kirby."

"Impressive. Who's the first-best sniffer?"

"The bloodhound." I open the door of the car and slide Bogart from my lap to the passenger seat. "I'll be right back." I leave Kirby and Bogart in their boy/dog face-off and scurry down my driveway.

My grandma Livia is no doubt at the kitchen table—her white hair still coiled around curlers—buried in her *People* magazine with a pasty bowl of oatmeal in front of her. A funneling tornado couldn't pull her away from celebrity gossip.

I scramble up the dilapidated wooden steps that lead to the room above the garage, and unlock the door.

I'd like to think we all have an inner geek. That, really, the geek is just the part of us that we fear no one

13

will accept, so we keep her a secret. There is not enough space in my dinky bedroom for my inner geek. She prefers the ample square footage in this room above the garage.

Save for a futon; a stereo system with turntable; five boxes of record albums; Fu-Fu, my Chinese Foo dog; a few stacks of my back issues of *The Bark* magazine; and a first-edition copy of Dad's debut book, *The Manifesto of Dog*, the room is empty.

This is where I nurture my inner geek, where she sings along with the voices on Dad's records. Where she looks at herself in the mirror, pretending to be outgoing, and says things like "Hi! I'm Natalie!" My cheeks totally puff up like beach balls when I say it, which is a good enough reason to avoid introducing myself to people—guy people. (Like, say for example, Taylor Newcastle, who unfortunately just graduated. Missed opportunity. Story of my life.)

I have to do all this singing, impersonating, and geeking with the door open, since Mom doesn't condone closed doors, but having the room to myself is worth it.

I don't have permission to sleep here or be in here after Mom goes to bed at night, but she said I might be able to start fixing it up this summer, a privilege earned by sweating for good grades and major begging the past couple of months.

As always, when I first enter the room, I reach

down and pet Fu-Fu, the cement Foo dog that Dad sent me from China a few years ago. He was on the Chinese leg of his book tour promoting *The Manifesto of Dog: Jui-wan tzen da chuan-lai suo-tser* (The Most Complete Dog Manual) in Chinese. Fu-Fu is actually part beast, part dog and is said to cultivate success and repel evil. This is reason enough for me to rub her enthusiastically each time I walk through the door. I would put a saddle on her and gallop her around the room if I knew it would bring me good luck, but I'm not that desperate. Yet.

I change into my jeans (low at the hip), pluck a fresh beige T-shirt (of the mother-approved shows-no-skin-above-the-waistline-variety) from my backpack, and deodorize. I grab a bag of dry dog food from underneath the sink in the small bathroom and make it back to Kirby, who drives us toward Highway 101.

Bogart's muzzle rummages inside the bag of food. "I have one more huge favor to ask."

"Yes?" Kirby says, deepening his voice.

"Could you watch him?" My mom will freak if I walk into the clinic with another dog. "Paco's always at the shop, right?" Paco is a fluffy Pomeranian and very much Eve's second child. He looks like a furry Russian hat with legs and two shiny black button eyes.

Kirby looks at Bogart, who removes his nose from the bag and crunches his food in slow motion while slobbering onto my jeans. "Fine." Much like a

Pekingese, Kirby can be profoundly stubborn, but his loyalty and friendship always shine through in the end. "I'm sure Paco and Bogart will have a blast sniffing each other's balls."

I laugh. "Paco's neutered, you know that, right?"

"Just a figure of speech." Bogart burps. Kirby plugs his nose. "My mom saves the orphans of the clothing world and you save dogs. You two were sisters in another life, I swear."

Kirby's mom and I are a lot alike. We both believe in second chances.

To a dog, the ultimate reprimand is its owner's lack of response.

—Michael Kaplan, *The Manifesto of Dog*

When I get to work and walk through the reception area, Hudson, a squat Welsh corgi, charges my leg and begins humping my ankle at high-impact-cardio speed.

"Sorry, he's been frisky lately," says Mrs. Palmer. An owner will always defend her pet.

The phone rings. I reach down and grab Hudson's little springlike legs, pry them off me, and lunge behind the reception desk. "Dr. Kaplan's office," I answer.

"Hi. I need to talk to you." Mom is only fifteen feet away from me, in her office, but leaning her head out the door would be unprofessional. It's important to be professional. I've heard this so many times that I'm convinced there is a country called Professional with its own formal lingo and food.

"Your first patient is here," I tell her.

"I know. I let them in. Go ahead and tell Mrs. Palmer I'll be with them shortly and come on back."

Hudson is now snuggled like a thick sausage between the loaves of Mrs. Palmer's arms. His triangular ears perk up as I walk toward him. Being a pushover, I scratch him under his chin. "She'll be with you in a moment."

Mom's office is covered with the blue ribbons of the veterinary world: plaques, gold seals, and letters from thankful clients with tagalong pictures—hundreds of pictures of dogs. Wide-eyed toy breeds coyly posing for the camera in winter sweaters. Sporting breeds, all sinew and muscle, planted in fields sloping toward points of interest outside the eye of the camera.

Mom's the vet. Dad, ten years her senior, is the behaviorist. They started a practice together after Mom completed vet school. Just dogs. Mom was in charge of administering vaccines, tending to wounds, and conducting routine checkups, but Dad shifted his focus from veterinarianism to psychoanalysis, conditioning dogs to listen and change their digging-holes-in-the-backyard ways. He was so good at it that people with money started calling. Soon enough, Dad was flying first class to New York and Miami to train and counsel their dogs. They call him the Dog Guru.

Mom swivels around in her tall chair behind her desk. Her long peppered gray hair is pulled back from her face with the only clip I've ever known her to have. She slides her glasses down the perfectly chiseled nose I did not inherit and motions me to sit on one of the vinyl chairs facing her desk. I plop down.

"How was the slumber party?" she asks.

"Fine," I reply, knowing that Mom will push for details.

"What did you do?" Bingo.

"Played a zillion rounds of charades, talked, ate ice cream straight from the carton—you know, girl stuff," I answer. Last spring was fashionably honest, so I quickly tally the lie that evolved from Maryann's slumber party and deposit it into the empty spring account.

"Good." Mom folds her hands on her desk. "Remember my friend Faith, my roommate from Tufts?"

"She was the lady with the ferret." A snapshot of a woman standing in our old kitchen, holding a tea-kettle in one hand and a scrawny black ferret in the other, comes to mind.

"That's her, yes. Good memory." I lap up the warm, creamy praise. "She came to visit about eight years ago." Mom clears her throat. "A few years before your father left."

My dad left Mom, Grandma Livia, our three dogs, and me the Thanksgiving of my sixth-grade year. "Left" is an understatement. Dads never just leave. My Dad left us for Hollywood, an answering service, a publicist, and a booking agent. Worst of all, he left us for some woman whose poodle had a piddling problem. Can't compete with that. He left big.

Now single, Dad devotes himself to spreading his gospel of dog internationally. He's spent the past month in England conducting seminars. At the end of this month, he's heading to Germany for his *Sprechen Sie Hund?* series. I see him only a handful of times throughout the year, and this summer I'll have to rely on postcards and long-distance calls from hotel rooms to let me know that my dad is still out there, thinking of me.

Mom leans forward and unclasps her hands. "Do you remember Faith's little boy?"

"He's the kid who gave Troy chocolate! Of course I remember him." Enter the vision of a freckled boy befriending my pug, Troy. Troy loved this kid. Followed him around. Slept in the guest room with him. And what did my sweet, teensy-muzzled, wrinkle-headed, curly-tailed Troy get in return from that stupid kid? An entire handful of poisonous chocolate chips! No one knew that the kid had given Troy the morsels until my poor pup started vomiting. Good thing Troy threw up all over Mom's Persian rug, because had he not, he probably would have died. Mom practically force-fed Troy burnt toast. It took a good week for him to get back to normal.

"I told Faith that her son could work here this summer. You can help me familiarize him with the clinic." There it is, so Mom-esque, short and to the point.

"But I have summer school from eight o'clock to noon every day, remember? I don't think I'll have time to babysit."

"Natalie, he's a year older than you. He just graduated from high school."

"Oh." Stupid, stupid, stupid. "He graduated at seventeen?"

"He skipped a grade in junior high." Lucky. "His score on the SAT was in the top one percent of his class." Great, another standard for me to live up to. "He was also granted early admission into Purdue. He's postponing college for a semester so that he can accompany Faith on her Physicians for Humanitarianism mission to Africa this fall."

My mother may have but one weakness: she worships all things scholarly. Anything that smells remotely academic gets inducted into the imaginary Hall of Fame erected in her head. I can only hope to click my heels and see it for myself someday.

One thing is clear: Boy Wonder's ignorance of the dangers of giving a dog chocolate is completely overshadowed by his recent academic endeavors. "Why would he want to come here?" I ask.

"To work. He's interested in veterinary science."

"Aren't there veterinarians where he lives?"

Mom's eyes widen in offense. "What's wrong with you?" she says, sounding disappointed. "It's the least I can do for Faith. Her son wants some hands-on experience. In return, I get some extra help around here." That is a low blow. I am a dedicated employee! Why would she need more help? "He'll be staying with us," Mom adds, as if this is an unexpected perk.

"Where?"

"In the room above the garage."

Snap! I want to leap out of my chair and scream. Mom said I could start fixing up that room this summer. That it could be my space.

Once again, I bite my tongue, accept Mom's decision like it's a heaping spoonful of sticky red cough syrup that I've no choice but to swallow. I hate her right now and slump into my chair.

"Stop pouting." Mom looks at her watch and stands up behind her desk. "Remember, you're driving Grandma to rummy tonight. I'll need to stay here until Vernon gets back. He's going to be gone all day." Vernon is Mom's assistant and lives on the premises, since we have dogs boarding in the clinic around the clock. "He'll give me a ride home." She leans over to kiss my forehead and smooth my hair.

Mom walks out the door and I feel as if a Chesapeake Bay retriever has dropped a load of disappointment into my lap. It's so heavy, I can't even stand up.

Just last month Mom wouldn't let me attend Nina's "Go Hollywood!" birthday extravaganza. Nina's older brother Jeffrey drove her and Kirby two hours north to Hollywood in her grandparents' motor home. Mom didn't think it was "age appropriate." I missed the walking tour of Sunset and Hollywood boulevards, getting lost in the Hollywood Hills while looking for Madonna's former mansion, and all the inside jokes that accompany such a trip.

Kirby and Nina did take a picture of Lassie's star on the Hollywood Walk of Fame for me, but still, I missed out on forming a firsthand memory of the entire experience.

Suddenly, a retrospective collection of photo album sleeves full of missed opportunities starts flipping in front of me. There're the "you're too young to fly alone" lost trip to New York City to see Dad on tour, the "not enough adult chaperones" missed sixth-grade class trip to Sacramento, the "it's too soon" veto of my driving alone thirty-two miles south to the ultimate dog beach with our three dogs the week I got my driver's license.

Mom is always saying I should be grateful for what

I have—the roof over my head and the food on the table. And I'm selfish, I know. But each time Mom puts her foot down, I lose something.

I'm beginning to wonder if it's not what we have but what we lose that matters most.

Inherently pack animals, dogs require the company of others.

—Michael Kaplan, *The Manifesto of Dog*

After work, I throw Mom's old Toyota Land Cruiser into reverse but remember that I've got Highway 101 behind me. A dramatic, lurching exit is impossible with the zoom of cars making their way along the hemline of the coast.

Beacon is a beach town, and its downtown is only about a quarter of a mile long, a blip of funky storefronts and cafés sandwiched between two bigger beach towns. Before the divorce, we lived inland, in a hollow tract house, host to hot, muggy summers.

When Dad left us for the "other" woman, the one with the peeing poodle, Mom hid herself in her bedroom for an entire three weeks. On the last day of her self-imposed confinement, she emerged a wild-haired, unshaven, robe-wearing cavewoman with an impulse. She threw open the door of her bedroom, marched into the den, where Grandma and I were watching *Entertainment Tonight,* stood on a stack of newspapers piled in front of us, and exclaimed, "We're moving to the beach!" It was the first and last time I saw Mom exercise spontaneity and bad hygiene.

We moved only forty-five minutes from familiarity and friends, but it felt like we had landed on a different continent: fog replaced smog, coastline understudied for the brown hilltops we'd once known, and outdoor farmers' markets took the place of poorly lit grocery stores with aisles displaying processed food. Oh, how I miss Cheez Whiz.

After we moved, it didn't take long for Mom to assume the control panel Dad had once manned. Perhaps she regretted not having kept her husband on a shorter leash, because she tightened the one on me, conveniently forgetting the reward segment of Pavlov's dog experiments.

An opening in the traffic allows me to join the pulse of cars and head toward Rescued Threads, a block away. I still have a half hour before I need to get Grandma.

I park along the street and rush toward the store through oncoming traffic.

From outside the shop, I see Kirby's mom in the front window. She's shoving the torso of a male mannequin into a Hawaiian shirt with a busy orange flower-and-pineapple pattern.

"Natalie!" Eve says as I walk into the shop. Carousels of color-coded clothes from decades past and present wait to be adopted. It's the humane society of clothing.

Eve is heavily scarved and jeweled in bangles that clink as she slides a stiff mannequin arm through the remaining sleeve of the Hawaiian shirt. "Prop him up, will you? I want to run outside and see what he looks like in the window." I put my arms out, not sure how to receive him. "Here, slide your hands up underneath his shirt in the back there."

I huddle behind the mannequin and feel odd that I notice his bare mannequin shoulder blades. They are tight and muscular. How pathetic is it that I'm groping a plastic man?

"Okay, right there!" Eve rushes outside to take a look and runs back in. "All this cabana boy needs is a hat." I'm a little disappointed that I have to relinquish him but feel somewhat relieved that I've found my backup boy should I need a date for prom next year.

Eve fits him with a straw hat and he's the leading man of the window display until a better one comes along.

Bogart emerges from behind the cash register counter on the other side of the store and waddles over to me. Paco is close behind. Bogart looks bald next to Paco's long, poufy-haired body. "Oh, Natalie," Eve says, "this guy is amazing. Paco is in heaven." She reaches down and lifts Bogart, who sags like an old, heavy pillow in her arms. He licks her face and she lets him. "Who does he belong to?"

"Someone who doesn't deserve him." I haven't quite figured out what I'm going to do about Bogart. The top priority right now is for him to get some good tender lovin' care. "Do you think you could watch him for a while longer?"

"Say no more." Eve sets Bogart down. He and Paco disappear into a round rack of vintage dresses.

"Kirby and Nina are in the back. If you'd been here any sooner, I bet you could have stopped them. You're the rational one."

"What are they doing?" I ask.

"I haven't seen the finished product, but go take a look."

I walk to the back of the store and push my way through the heavy red velvet curtain, toward the blare of what sounds like a blow drier coming from the bathroom.

"It's me!" I yell, pounding on the locked door.

"Just a sec!" Nina shouts back. I lean against the wall. I'll wait. Nina might have abandoned me last night, but there was a time when she saved me.

I moved here the summer before seventh grade. During the first weeks of junior high, I got by on my own at school, avoiding any possible eye contact (a basic survival instinct of the shy and introverted).

PE became the hell pit of my day. There is no place to hide in PE. It's the closest thing ever to being naked in public. Kirby was in my PE class. He was lanky and pimply, and he had the signature changing voice of boys his age. His black-rimmed glasses, perhaps cool in high school, set off a nerd alarm in junior high. He had to wear a thick black strap around his head in PE to keep the glasses from falling off. That caused him further disgrace and made him the target of the eighth-grade wedgie brigade.

Kirby was much more consumed with biting his nails than looking anyone in the eye.

We were the slowest runners on our Friday cross-country laps. One Friday, during a run, I tripped over a protruding tree root on the sidewalk and fell. Kirby stopped, helped me up, and asked if I was okay.

After that, we started eating lunch together in his spot: against the chain-link fence bordering the parking lot. He was obsessed with the Beatles and J.R.R. Tolkien books. I was obsessed with James Herriot novels and the Westminster Kennel Club Dog Show. I even told him my secret about belonging to the American Kennel Club under the pseudonym Nan Tuckers. Not even my mom knows that.

With each other we found the confidence to be ourselves without worrying about being judged or criticized. But in the larger world, Kirby kept biting his nails and I kept my head down.

Then Nina came along. Military kid hopping from town to town. She'd returned to the United States after her dad had been stationed in France for two years. Bold and resilient yet gentle and lovable, she held the essence of an Irish setter.

Nina wore pink Converse high-tops in our PE class and actually made the PE uniform look cool. Sometimes during those Friday laps, she would sprint to the front of the pack because she could, but more often than not, she ran slowly with Kirby and me.

She forced us to eat lunch at a lunch table, made us read Jim Morrison lyrics, and taught us French endearments like *"mon petit chou,"* which means "my little cabbage." She swears people say that.

Any clique at school would have allowed Nina in, but for some reason, she chose Kirby and me. Being in the front of a line or in clear view of others didn't scare her. We were right there with her but always were—and still are—within the edges of her shadow.

"Are you ready?" Kirby asks from inside the bathroom, snapping me to attention.

I move away from the wall. "For what? I've got to tell you something and I don't have much time."

The door squeaks open to reveal Nina and Kirby standing side by side with hair the hue of a blue ribbon one might find on a winning science fair project (never my science fair project).

"Ta-da!" Nina shouts. "What do you think?" She shakes her head, allowing her once auburn hair to dangle its blue below her shoulders. Kirby pokes his fingers through his straggly hair. "Are you in?" Nina asks.

"No way."

Nina seems hurt. "Is this because of last night?"

"What do you mean?"

"I mean, are you holding back because you're mad at me?"

"Of course not." I want to tell her I don't get how she could even think of Laney, Maryann, and those other girls as friends. But I would only sound jealous. And maybe I am.

"I thought we should branch out a little, Nat. And where did you disappear to, by the way?"

"The backyard. What? You weren't part of the team that ornamented me with bras?"

"No." She lets out a giggle.

"Yeah," I say with a straight face, "hilarious."

"Did you have any fun at all?" she asks.

"Um, let me think. . . . No."

Nina grabs my hands like we're two schoolgirls on the playground. "Now, c'mon, Nattie! It's only hair. The dye will fade. Just for the summer."

Kirby holds a rope of my long wavy brown hair in his hand. "You don't even have to go all blue; just do a strand or two."

Kirby and Nina don't have to worry about what

their mothers will think, but my mom would be furious if I came home with a head full of blue hair. She held out on letting me get my ears pierced until I turned fourteen, and even then, I was limited to one hole per lobe—studs, no hoops. Distressed jeans with cool holes and scrape marks are banned from my closet because Mom thinks they look trashy and it is mortifying to her that anyone would pay money for a pair of ruined jeans. I barely squeak by with the faded ones I wear. I doubt Mom would approve of blue hair.

Maybe it's because I spent an inordinate amount of time today harboring resentment toward my mother, but I feel the desire to rebel. I should dye my hair. Or shave it all off.

"Okay, go for it. All of it! Dye my eyebrows, too." Kirby hurries to grab a box of hair color obviously reserved for me.

"Wait," I say. Mom will disembowel me. This is not rebellion. This is plain stupid. "Don't dye all of it. Just do this section in the front. On the right side."

Nina drapes a towel over my shoulders and tilts my head forward into the sink, dunking it gently under the faucet.

A few minutes later, the cord of hair I surrendered is emblazoned in blue. As I stand in front of the mirror, tears overflow from my brown eyes and skitter down my round cheeks, then cliff-dive toward my narrow body below. The blue is not too dramatic: most of my head is still covered with a mane of wavy brown hair.

"What's wrong?" Kirby asks.

"We can dye it back if you want," Nina says, grasping my shoulders.

I sniffle. "It's not the hair." I trudge over to the toilet and sit. Nina and Kirby crouch at my knees. "It's my mom. This guy is moving in with us."

"I didn't know she had a boyfriend," Kirby says.

"No, it's this guy our age. He's the son of some lady my mom went to college with," I explain. "The lady had a ferret and the son almost killed my dog Troy with chocolate." Nina unravels some toilet paper from the roll and dabs my cheeks. "He gets the room above the garage."

Nina and Kirby recoil and gasp sympathetically.

"Why is he coming to live with you?" Nina asks.

"Because he likes animals. And he cranked on his SATs." I wipe my nose along the back of my hand. "And he's traveling to Africa to help his mom cure people."

"I'm sorry, Nattie," Nina says. "I was looking forward to helping you fix up that room this summer. I was even getting used to the open-door policy."

I shake my head. "The guy is probably just an older version of his stupid former self with a bookshelf full of Cliff's Notes who got lucky and aced high school." I tear a sequence of squares off the toilet paper roll and blow my nose. "Unlike me, who totally sweats my ass off to score a report card that looks like a tribute to the first letter of the alphabet."

"Glass full. Glass full, okay?" Nina says in a calming voice. She springs up from the ground. "Glass full, he might be amazing. He could be totally hot and know all about black holes and the mysteries of the universe. Maybe he'll know how to clip bonsai trees."

Kirby adds, "Maybe he collects belly button lint for his loom so he can weave elaborate wall hangings. Or"—Kirby pauses to run his fingers through his mop top once again—"maybe he has blue hair."

Auditory signals enhance obedience training sessions. —Michael Kaplan, *The Manifesto of Dog*

It's already past five-thirty. I'm late, and Grandma will not understand. I jet out of Rescued Threads and zoom home across train tracks, darting past the 7-Eleven parking lot, which buzzes with skateboarders, and into Residentia.

When I get home, Grandma is standing as still as a hood ornament on the curb. I step out to help her even though, at seventy-eight, she insists she can do things on her own.

She wears her fitted pin-striped blazer and skirt. A pile of silver hair perches atop her head like a tidy bird's nest. Her swollen feet manage to squeeze into the daintiest of shoes. Tonight she's forced them into black patent leathers.

Standing at the open passenger door, she glares at

me from behind an army of wrinkles. "You are late," she says in her thick German accent, leaning over to kiss me on the cheek.

"Hi, Grandma. I'm only eight minutes late tonight."

She lifts herself into the seat and clutches her purse on her lap as if she's holding on to a roller coaster bar.

Once she's secured inside, I get behind the wheel and restart the car. "You look nice."

Grandma stares at me, her brow furrowed. "Vhat did you do to your hair? You look like a girl on the MTV." As if MTV is the dumping ground for all youth's derelicts.

I pull away from the curb and follow the curve of the cul-de-sac. "Keep your eyes on the voad." Grandma points a crooked finger toward the block ahead as we pass Laney's house again. She reaches toward the radio dial. "How do you turn this off?"

"It is off."

Grandma came to live with us after Grandpa died, a year before Dad left. If I could choose only one comparison between Grandma and my mom, it would be that Grandma's tyrannical disposition in the car is very similar to Mom's control-freak tendencies as a mother.

One might think that my mom is strict with me because she was raised by wolflike parents, but this is not true. Oddly enough, my mom breathed from a tank of freedom when she was my age. My grandparents trusted her. She got to live with a host family in Spain

36

for a semester when she was sixteen. My mom would never let me have that kind of experience, even with a surveillance camera sewn into my skull.

My current theory is that Mom doesn't trust me because she has the brain of a forty-five-year-old woman whose ex-husband, although firm and controlled with dogs, has no control over the unit located in his boxer shorts. Therefore, Mom thinks I don't have the self-control needed to contain myself should I be in a position where I am asked to do something dangerous or profane—like drink cheap wine or flash my boobs.

"Turn on blinker!" Grandma shouts when we reach Clove Street. I am taking driving cues from a woman who survived the Holocaust but never managed to pass her driver's test.

"Grandma, we need to go one more block to Jade."

She starts knocking on the dashboard with a fist. "Here! Turn here!"

I heed her directions the rest of the ride even though it takes triple time to get to the senior center.

When we arrive, she asks, "Are you coming in?"

"No, thanks." I reach behind the seat, where Mom told me she'd put my U.S. History book. "Class starts on Monday, and I already have reading assigned." I talked Nina and Kirby into taking U.S. History with me this summer: four hours a day, five days a week for six weeks and we'll earn ourselves a free period next year.

"Good." She gives me a friendly slap on the knee.

"I tell everyone you are a good student, study hard. That you even go to school in the summer!" She leans over and I reach the rest of the way so that she can give me a kiss. Then she sobers her tone. "You stay here for me."

I watch my grandmother leave the car and shuffle slowly into the mouth of the senior center. My grandpa, a U.S. soldier, liberated her concentration camp, and later, they fell in love. She has lived through the loss of her parents and sisters, the pain of three miscarriages, and the death of her husband.

And here I am feeling sorry for myself.

History assignment for first class: read chapter 1, "Manifest Destiny."

Grandma must have played a good round of rummy, because an hour and a half later, on the drive home, I get only a few fist poundings on the dashboard from her. "Ve play rummy vhen ve get home. I show you how your grandmother von tonight," she says proudly.

When we get home, the house is dark. Mom must still be at the clinic.

Before I slip the key into the door, the dogs bark their excitement on the other side. Pip (golden retriever with one eye), Southpaw (velvety black Great Dane and Labrador mix missing her right foreleg), and Otto (German shepherd with parts intact) meet us.

"Go! Oafs!" Grandma says, waving them away from her space. They cower in her presence. Then she disappears into the kitchen as their tails begin to thump on the wall, sounding like the percussion section of a marching band.

I smooch each one of them. "Hi, babies."

They follow me into the kitchen. Grandma is at the counter, lifting the dome off a cake platter. "I made chocolate," she says, cutting into the soft moistness of the cake.

After replenishing food and water for the dogs and pouring hot water from the kettle into Grandma's tea-bagged mug, we play rummy at the kitchen table. She wins each round with black, white, and red fanned arrangements of same-suited sequences of hearts, clubs, diamonds, and spades. "Vone more?" she asks after my many losses. "You vill vin this time."

I will not win. Not now. I've already lost too much today with Mom taking my room away from me.

"No, thanks. I have to work tomorrow. Better get to bed." I kiss her good night and take our cake plates to the sink. "The cake was excellent, by the way."

Grandma's cakes are always perfect. She told me once that cake saved her life. When she was in the concentration camp, she and the other girls in her bunker were freezing, terrified, and starving. They would make up elaborate recipes for cake to distract them from the living hell they had to inhabit. "Sometimes imagination keeps us alive," she told me.

Instead of climbing the stairs to my bedroom, I risk walking out into the cool night and up the stairway to the room above the garage. The dogs follow me.

Inside, I bend down to rub Fu-Fu. I keep the room dark and walk to the window facing the street. A telescope isn't necessary for a perfect view of Laney Benning's porch, where Laney is now sitting in a lounge chair, looking past the lamppost. Her long sandy brown hair covers her bare shoulders like a shawl.

A red car pulls up in front of Laney's house. She stands, hesitates cautiously for a second, pulls a duffel bag from beneath her chair, then lugs it down the steps and into the car. A bass beat pours from the open door, then stops once the door is shut. The car follows the curve of the cul-de-sac. Its red taillights flicker and then fade down the block.

Laney reminds me of the women on the covers of Grandma's glossy magazines. I just don't get why I care what she's doing, yet I can't help flipping through the pages to find out.

**A game of catch awakens a dog's fundamental
need to retrieve.**

—Michael Kaplan, *The Manifesto of Dog*

Mom came into my room last night just before ten-thirty, kissed me on the forehead, and told me she was home. I was curled up in my bed with the lights out, putting off facing her with blue hair.

She goes in early on Saturdays, so I walk the mile and a half to work this morning.

To have my own car would be bliss—and not just because I could display a My Dog Is Smarter Than Your Honor Student bumper sticker on the fender. In the world according to Mom, giving me a car would be like providing me with a gateway drug. It might push me toward hard-core activities like shooting heroin, having sex, and driving myself to school.

But really, a car would be nice to have, especially because I'll be working every day after school and all day on Saturdays this summer: that is a lot of walking. The good news is that I'll clock in about thirty hours a week at $240 per week. By the end of summer, $2,000 will be mine to buy my own car with. Then will come the real work of convincing my mom to let me buy one. Baby steps, though.

When I get to work, I stand outside the window-paned door and see a guy in the reception area looking at the Dogs of the World poster on the wall. He turns to me when I push open the door and the bell on the handle jingles.

I've liked guys in the past but almost always from a distance. Like I'm holding binoculars and I can see them, but they can't see me. (As was the case with the recently departed Taylor Newcastle.)

There's something about this guy, though. I'm standing in the reception area, unable to blink. A tribal drum beats in the vault of my chest, and I'm feeling tingly all over. I mean, *all* over.

His blond hair is disheveled and slightly covers his light green eyes. I'd guess he's eighteen—nineteen, maybe. His face appears mature enough to have survived puberty but it's not whiskered and sharp like those of the older men in Grandma's *GQ* magazines. I'm enjoying his pink cheeks and boyish freckles. He may be a tad weather-beaten, but he carries a kindliness and self-confidence: very Portuguese water dog meets golden retriever.

"You must be your mom's daughter," he says to me.

Okay, so maybe he's not too bright.

He whacks his forehead with his palm. "That sounded pretty stupid." Perceptive. "I meant to say that you must be Dr. Kaplan's daughter."

"Natalie," someone else says. The voice is low and pissy. Maryann McClure stands a few feet away, show-casing her glossy globbed lips and tanning-booth radiance. A little pink purse dangles from her wrist. The bleach blond plume of hair surrounding her head makes her look scrawny. She is so hairless Chinese crested dog, it's not even funny. "Where's Bogart?" she snaps.

"I'm not ready to tell you." If she really cared, she would have been here yesterday.

Poster Boy looks from me to her. He's tall enough that my head would perfectly fit on his shoulder without my standing on my tiptoes. I take further stock of him, admiring his simple style: faded baggy jeans, white T-shirt, and black flip-flops. Definitely more "let's watch the sunset" than "I'm gonna go shoot me a bear!" A thick-banded watch hugs his wrist. It has one of those compass/stopwatch/time-telling faces that say something about a person, although I'm not sure what.

A pixie in my stomach does a backflip.

Maryann crosses her arms. "You were outside with

Bogart. He was sleeping next to you when we put our bras on your stomach." Great, Poster Boy must think I'm a real winner.

I narrow my eyes at her. "He had dirty water, no food. His nails were completely overgrown, which, by the way, can be harmful to a dog of his breed. He was clearly being neglected." Maryann looks at me long and hard, her lips puckered in frustration. Defeated, she leaves the office, bell jingling behind her.

Poster Boy gazes at me like I'm the superhero of the dog world. The temptation to place my fists on my waist in a photo-op pose, my hair swooping up behind me and a banner that says "Dog Girl!" waving over-head, evaporates quickly.

Reminder: breathe. I walk behind the reception desk for security. A blue strand of hair dangles over my eye. I wish I could tuck it into a drawer. Mom didn't see me last night, and I'm not looking forward to her reaction.

I need to ask Poster Boy why he's here: whether he has a dog in the exam room, whether he's here for a pickup, whether he has a girlfriend, whether he'd like a Shiatsu massage. "Are you waiting for someone?" I manage to ask.

He runs his hand along the back of his neck before shoving it into his pocket. "Actually, I'm waiting for your mom. She said she'd be right back."

Outside the pounding of the tom-tom in my chest, there's a bubble of silence. "Have you seen a dog like this?" He points to the bearlike Bouvier des Flandres, a relative of the massive Newfoundland, on the poster.

Mom pops out of the examination room. "It'll be just a few more minutes," she says, smiling at Poster Boy. Her smile fades when she sees me and my length of blue hair. I can tell in a millisecond that she is not happy. "Hey, Natalie, can I talk to you?"

I shouldn't have dyed my hair.

Mom tows me on an invisible rope into the exam room, leaving Poster Boy with his unanswered question. She shuts the door behind her and reaches out to finger my blue tendril of hair. "What is this?"

"Nina, Kirby, and I dyed our hair yesterday," I say, trying to convey sincere advocacy of blue hair.

"Well, it is unbecoming and completely inappropriate." Mom frowns, opens her mouth to proceed with more criticism, but I quickly change the subject.

"Who is that guy in the reception area?"

She leans against the stainless steel exam table, which is always cold to the touch. Fortunately, I've distracted her. "That's Faith's son. Carver." She says it as if "C-a-r-v-e-r" has been a part of our vocabulary for years.

"You didn't say he'd be here today."

"I would have told you yesterday, but you were so upset. Vernon picked him up from the airport and Carver stayed with him last night."

I eye the countertop with its glass jars of Q-tips,

cotton balls, and prepackaged syringes. Mom knew that Carver would be here today. She didn't tell me. Is that any different from lying?

She starts to get defensive. "We need the help now. Our patient load has increased and we always have more boarders during the summer."

Nice. As usual, I get to be told what is happening, as if my life is some story being written by my mother. There's no room for insertions or deletions.

"Be open to this, okay?" Mom brings me closer for a badly timed hug. I'm waiting for her to demand that I dye my blue-streaked hair back to brown. She doesn't say anything, though, which is unusual.

Is this an even trade? Mom sort of lied to me about Poster Boy, so maybe her gift to me is a stripe of blue hair. This may be the first gift from her that I've ever gotten to choose without her guidance. I certainly didn't choose the gifts she presented to me on my last birthday, including the book *What Smart Students Know: Maximum Grades. Optimum Learning. Minimum Time.*, which may very well be a riveting read. I was just too busy studying to crack it open.

Mom releases me, and we step into the reception area. Carver is still there, but he's crouched in front of Duke, a miniature Yorkshire terrier. The little guy is a lapdog with a tremendous amount of long silky steel blue hair. A plaid bow adorns his small flat head. Evidently, Duke is secure enough in his manhood to wear hair accessories. He sits on the leg of his owner,

46

Mrs. Lewis, and licks Carver's hand: proof that Carver has already won him over.

I watch closely in case Carver has a bag of chocolate chips hiding under his shirt.

Duke stops licking Carver and perks up his ears as Vernon ducks through the front door. Vernon looks like a piece of artwork: bronzed, with a perfectly smooth gleaming bald head. He's middle-aged but working his way through college so that he can go to vet school.

"Hey, Nattie!" With a hand big enough to hold a litter of cocker spaniel puppies, he balances four carry-out coffee cups in a cardboard holder. At the reception desk, he creates a coaster out of a napkin and sets one of the cups down. "For you, miss. The way you like it: slathered with whipped cream. Nice hair, by the way. Blue is your color."

"Thanks, Vernon." I smile.

Mom pulls back from her conversation with Duke and Mrs. Lewis to claim her cup, the only one with a string dangling on the outside. There must be an Earl Grey tea bag floating in there.

"Here's one for you, too, Carver," Vernon says. "No whipped cream, right?" No whipped cream? To deprive oneself of whipped cream is masochistic and wrong.

"Thanks." Carver grins. One of his eyeteeth is slightly crooked over another tooth, an appealing imperfection.

Focus.

"It's our Saturday ritual, right, Natalie?" I nod. Vernon walks over to Duke. "And how's this guy doing today?" Mrs. Lewis and Duke steer their saucer eyes to Vernon. "C'mon back," he says. The three of them disappear into the exam room.

Before Mom follows them, she says, "Carver, Natalie will show you around." It's terrific that Mom has finally given me permission to be alone with a guy, but he happens to be the guy who almost killed my beloved Troy. He's also swindling me out of my sacred space in the room above the garage.

Carver stands with one hand in his pocket and the other holding his no-whip hot chocolate. He rocks back and forth on his feet, waiting.

There is no reason I should take kindly to Carver. Mom brought him here against my better judgment, and although he is very attractive, bordering on hot, disliking him is the only way I can express how utterly pissed off I am at her for giving away my personal space. I didn't dye my hair completely blue, but I can exercise my free will by being a complete bitch.

It's settled, then.

I simply need to figure out how to walk backward from feeling drawn to Carver in the first place.

An enlightened owner knows that a dog must earn his respect. —Michael Kaplan, *The Manifesto of Dog*

Unbeknownst to me, the whipped cream underneath the lid of my cup has melted from the heat of the cocoa. I take a sip and it sears my tongue. "Ow!" I shout. Cocoa spurts out my mouth and onto my beige shirt.

"You okay?" Carver asks. My teeth clamp down on my tongue. I nod but know I look like a reject in a wet T-shirt contest. It occurs to me that I should have paid attention to the clothes in my closet this morning instead of grabbing a limp shirt from the floor. (When I sniffed it, I ignored the slight smell of yesterday on it.)

Carver walks toward me and holds out a napkin. Maybe it's because I live with a grandmother who has no qualms about charging at a stained shirt with a napkin and rubbing the spot until the napkin turns to shreds, but I signal him with my hand to stop. Carver takes a few steps back, still holding the napkin out to me. "Thought you'd want this."

"No, thanks."

His helpful hand falls to his side. Afraid of another outburst, I plunk my hot chocolate onto the counter of the reception desk, cross my arms over my strawberry fields, and try to shift the conversation to more important matters. "So do you own a dog?" I need to make sure it's safe for him to work here.

"No," Carver says, looking perplexed by my very clear and straightforward question.

Oh, wait a minute.

I get it.

He must like cats, in which case he is completely out of line. One cannot be both a dog person and a cat person; to suggest love for both implies compromise.

Carver takes what looks like a strong yet soft hand out of his pocket and scratches his ear. Perhaps he's allergic to the sizable amount of dog hair in the room. I'm waiting for him to sneeze.

He doesn't.

"Is something wrong?" he asks.

"Well, it's just that my mom specializes in dogs. She doesn't treat cats, or birds, even. Just dogs. Are you okay with that?" I ask with sincere curiosity.

"I don't own a dog now. He died about three months ago."

"I'm sorry." I wonder what kind of dog it was and how it died.

"I do have fish," Carver says with a touch of pride.

"Excuse me?" Did he say *fish*? A fish is not a pet. People eat fish. Grill it. Panfry it.

Carver walks a bit closer to me. I lean back against the high-topped counter. He says, "Koi. I've worked at the San Francisco Botanical Garden the past couple of years and helped take care of them." He squints with suspicion. "Have you ever seen a koi?"

"Aren't they, like, carp, or something?" Please tell me why anyone would own or care for carp. They are bottom-feeders. It's like having a dung beetle for a pet.

"Yeah, they're a type of carp." Carver's eyes light up, as if there are birthday candles in front of him and he's picturing the wish he's going to make. "Koi are amazing animals."

I heartily disagree. There are no Seeing Eye fish or Civil War fish. I don't recall a fish ever changing the course of history, like a fish on a mission to the moon or a fish leading people in life rafts away from the sinking *Titanic*.

Carver reads my skepticism. "Koi are intelligent. Loyal. Do you know they can live to be two hundred years old?"

Of course a fish is going to be loyal. It's in a tank, for crying out loud! It's certainly not going to jump

51

out if it's unhappy with you. And you want loyalty? Take a look at the Lab who guided her owner from the seventy-eighth floor of the World Trade Center to safety on 9/11. That is loyalty.

The office phone rings. I bound behind the desk to answer it.

While I pencil in an appointment for Helga, a greater Swiss mountain dog who is experiencing a recent change in behavior—from independent to clingy—Carver boldly opens the door to the supply closet next to Mom's office and extracts a broom.

I pretend not to notice him, but the bristles against the tile floor swoosh in rhythm with the loud drumming in my chest, the rapid beat of my stupid heart.

Ensure that your home is dogproof by touring it on all fours. —Michael Kaplan, *The Manifesto of Dog*

Saturday is our busiest day, so Carver never gets an official tour of the clinic. He spends most of the morning and afternoon shadowing Vernon but is not allowed to go into the kennel area, where the dogs are kept.

This should give Carver an accurate glimpse of my mother's personality. A reputable SAT score may buy you a ticket to Elizabeth Kaplan's makeshift veterinary internship program and allow you to gain full access to her daughter's sacred space, but it's not the open sesame into the kennel run.

After work, Vernon helps load the back of the Land Cruiser with Carver's bulging black duffel bags. I hesitantly hand over my key to the room above the garage to Mom, who gives it to Carver—a transaction

I've been dreading, made more painful by its happening sooner than I thought it would.

Mom drives us home, Carver in the back, me in the front. I'm self-conscious about what he might think of my dull profile, but I remind myself that this is someone who not only may have a secret affinity for cats, but also has a verified adoration of fish.

At home we're met by the dog entourage. Carver pushes through the door, fearless. With full force, Otto sniffs his crotch. "Ohhhhhh-kay, buddy," Carver says.

"Settle!" Mom's voice is firm and effective. Even Carver and I stand a little straighter. Otto pulls back and sits. Southpaw and Pip can barely lasso in their excitement, but they also obey Mom's command.

"Natalie, why don't you take them out?"

"It's okay," Carver says. "They're just excited."

"Go ahead and put them out, Natalie," Mom says again. "Don't want you to be too overwhelmed, Carver." She is actually considering Carver's feelings. I sprouted from this woman's loins; where is the consideration for *my* feelings?

"Who is there?" Grandma yells from the kitchen in a shrill voice. The smell of Swiss cheese and nutmeg wafting toward us softens the blow.

I herd the dogs out back and return to the kitchen, where Grandma takes a casserole smothered in melted cheese out of the oven. She wears the apron I gave her about ten years ago that reads "I love gamdda." My small smudgy handprint is still on it. Carver leans in and offers to shake Grandma's oven-mitted hand. "I'm Carver. Nice to meet you."

She gives him a head-to-toe-and-back-again scan. "Dinner is ready."

We settle into our chairs around the table. Carver sits between Mom and Grandma. Mom brandishes her napkin at her side until it lowers like a parachute onto her lap. "I'm sure you'll find that the biggest perk of living here is my mother's cooking." Thanks for the vote of confidence, Mom.

The dogs start barking outside. Someone knocks at the door. "I'll get it," I say.

I open the door, and Maryann McClure's mother is standing there in a peach pantsuit with corresponding nail polish. The likeness between Maryann and her mother is shocking. Namely the glossed lips and the gum-smacking mouth. "Hi, Mrs. McClure." I'm fearing for my life right now.

"May I speak to your mother, please?" If Fu-Fu were here, I'd be rubbing my fingers to the bone. Is this about Maryann's slumber party? Is Mom going to find out there was no parental supervision there? I didn't lift my shirt or swig wine, but I'm feeling guilty, doomed.

Mom approaches, wiping her hands on her napkin. "Who is it?" I step to the side.

"Your daughter stole our dog," Mrs. McClure says accusingly.

Relief. This is about Bogart. Mom looks at me, confused.

"He's at Kirby's house," I explain.

A pained expression spreads across Mom's face. "You stole her dog?"

I ignore her question. "I'm sorry, Mrs. McClure, but Bogart was in need of food and water."

Mrs. McClure crosses her arms over her well-endowed chest. Her gum chewing becomes more rapid. "Are you trying to say we don't take care of our own dog?" She wasn't home the night of Maryann's party, so I'd go further to say that she doesn't have the radar on her daughter, either.

"Will you excuse us for a moment, Mrs. McClure?" Mom asks. Mrs. McClure busies herself with her gum while Mom pulls me into the living room. "What are you doing?"

"Mom, the dog was neglected. You've always taught me to care for animals that need it. I was just doing the right thing."

Mom gives me a sideways glance. "You could have called the humane society."

"Like we did with Pip?"

"We found Pip, Natalie."

"Yeah, in someone's yard."

She glares at me. "He was abused. Bleeding."

I follow her back to the front door, where Mrs. McClure is checking her cuticles. "Sorry about this," Mom says, as if I've done something wrong. Humph.

"Natalie, call Kirby and let him know that Mrs. McClure is coming to get her dog."

I give Mrs. McClure directions to Kirby's house and call to tell him that he'll have to return Bogart. There is no such thing as a quick phone call to Kirby if you catch him excited about something. This time it's a video game. "I kicked royal ass in *Resident Evil*, Natalie. I beat my own towering top score!"

After the phone call, I pass Grandma in the living room watching Bobby Flay grill sea bass on TV: one example of how people in this world regard fish.

I find Mom in the kitchen. No sign of Carver.

Mom doesn't notice me in the doorway just yet. She sits at the kitchen table gently petting Southpaw, whose head is snuggled in Mom's lap. Mom bends down and kisses Southpaw's head. Southpaw nudges her muzzle closer to Mom's belly. Mom tenderly rubs her ears. "Good girl."

That is all I've ever wanted to hear from Mom. And she just said it to the dog—who is simply breathing and being a dog. Southpaw does not have to earn an A on an algebra test, walk through the door before curfew, or drive Grandma to the senior center. She gets to be told that she's a good girl for existing.

I should be ashamed of myself for feeling jealous as I watch Mom dote on Southpaw, but there is honestly nothing more I want in the world than to have Mom tell me that I'm a good girl without my having to do anything but be myself.

I clear my throat and get Mom's attention. Southpaw trots over to me for a quick pat on the head.

Mom rinses off the dishes and puts them in the dishwasher while I finish my dinner. She doesn't mention the scene with Mrs. McClure. Perhaps deep down she knows I did the right thing by taking Bogart. I wish she would tell me when I do something right. More often than not, I know I've done something right when she doesn't say anything. She sure doesn't bite her tongue when I do something wrong.

Mom leans over the sink to scrub it. "Carver went upstairs to his room," she says, as if I'm wondering where he is.

"I'm going to get my albums." They are rightfully mine. Mom can't argue with that.

"Be quick about it, then," she says. "He's probably eager to settle in." Mom turns away from the sink and faces me with a sponge still gripped in her hand. "I do want to make sure we're clear about this, though."

This can't be good. "Clear about what?"

"Boundaries. Carver is a guest in our home." This is all she needs to say for me to understand fully. She is telling me in Momspeak that if I should attempt to jump Carver's bones, she will annihilate me.

Here I am again, on the Ferris wheel of Mom's trust issues. I really wonder if Dad knows how much his affair has ruined my life.

* * *

Standing at the door to the room above the garage, I can hear music from the other side. Elton John. "Benny and the Jets."

Carver's found Dad's records—ahem, *my* records.

Good. Now it's my turn to take something from him.

A dog derives meaning through its sense of smell. —Michael Kaplan, *The Manifesto of Dog*

When Mom and Dad split, Dad wanted me to have his albums and turntable. After we moved here, I set up Dad's stereo in the room above the garage. I'd listen to record after record, trying to decode the message I thought Dad was leaving me. The voices of Joni Mitchell, David Bowie, and Cat Stevens grew on me, but I still felt lost inside the lyrics. Which was Dad's song to me?

I take a deep breath and knock, then cough from holding my breath too long.

Carver opens the door in the middle of my coughing fit. "Let me get you some water." He waves me in and shuts the door behind him. (He obviously hasn't read Mom's rule book regarding closed doors.) Despite my coughing, I reach down and pet Fu-Fu while Carver gets me a drink, as if I'm a guest in his room.

After five Dixie cups of tap water, the hacking stops. Carver walks over to the stereo and turns the volume down.

Seeing someone in this room hurts my stomach. I look around at the record player, the books on the shelf, the stacks of magazines: it's only a room, I guess. But when I'm in here alone, it's so much more than that.

"I was hoping there'd be music," says Carver. He must have seen the old turntable and headed straight for the boxes of albums, because his duffel bags are still lumped on the floor, unopened. "I only have my iPod, which is fine, but I didn't expect there'd be speakers. And albums! It's like I've walked into the ultimate anachronism." Anachro-what? Bet that's an SAT word.

I wrap my arms around myself even though it's not cold. "Yeah, my dad left those for me."

"Oh, that's right." Carver's eyebrows dip sympathetically. "Sorry." His mom must have told him about Dad's fling.

"Yeah, well. I'm gonna take the albums out of your way."

"Out of my way? This collection is amazing. Led Zeppelin, Ella Fitzgerald, Nick Drake."

"It won't take me long to get my stuff." I say this like we're divorced and I've come to get my things. I grab *The Manifesto of Dog*, by Dad, from the bookshelf. It's a hardback with a red cover lettered in gold.

"What's that?" Carver asks.

"A book my dad wrote."

Carver nods. "My mom said he's a dog aficionado."

"The Dog Guru," I say, correcting him. With the thick book in my hand, I go to box number one of five filled with records. I put the book on top of the box and squat down in an attempt to lift it. Of course, it weighs a thousand pounds, so I can't even move it. How humiliating.

Carver leans down on the opposite side of the box. "I'll help you."

"No, that's okay." He's less than a ruler's length away from me. I notice that his eyes are not light green but, more specifically, olive green. I can feel the pixie on the performance mat in my stomach. "It's just going to take me a few trips."

I straighten up and walk empty-handed toward the door. "I'll get this first," I say, hoisting up Fu-Fu. I'm disappointed that she didn't ward off the intruder who happens to be hypnotizing Pixie right now.

"I can help," Carver offers again. Does he have to be so freaking nice?

"No," I say, more firmly this time.

I realize I am stroking Fu-Fu behind the ear and immediately stop, hoping Carver doesn't disregard my tough-girl facade because I was petting an inanimate object. I really am trying to be tough.

Carver scratches his head as if he's confused—or has fleas (doubtful, I know). "Well, I'll leave the door open for you," he says.

I start down the steps with Fu-Fu. Her sharp cement ear is practically poking up my left nostril. I get the feeling someone is staring. Peeking over Fu-Fu, I see Laney Benning on her porch. What a turnabout. Now she's watching me.

Dogs differ from wolves because of their dependence on man. —Michael Kaplan, *The Manifesto of Dog*

With each load of records I carried last night, Carver would make another stack at the bottom of the stairs so I wouldn't have to climb all the way up to the room. At first I thought it was a considerate gesture, but then I realized he might have been trying to get me out of his silky, perfectly floppy hair. I'm still on the fence about it.

Aside from taking the dogs for numerous walks, I stay holed up in my tiny yellow bedroom on Sunday, redecorating. My bedroom is the size of Nina's walk-in closet. In SAT analogy–speak: ROOM ABOVE THE GARAGE: 190-POUND ENGLISH MASTIFF :: MY BEDROOM : 5-POUND JAPANESE SPANIEL.

I can literally sit on the edge of my double bed and

open the door to my room with one foot and slide the door of my closet closed with the other. And now that I've emptied the contents of the room above the garage into my bedroom, it's even more claustrophobic. In the event of a Southern California earthquake, the chances of my survival are slight. Mom can burden the guilt of that one as far as I'm concerned.

My bedroom space is limited, but I do what I can, rearranging bookshelves and pushing my bed toward the opposite wall, where I can look out the window and have a clear view of the room above the garage.

Now that my bed is an observation deck, I plan to keep watch over the room in case Carver chooses to smuggle pickaxes and jackhammers up the stairs. He might turn out to be some good-looking rebel vandalizer from hell who hides behind a strong command of the English language. You just never know kids these days.

Whoa. I sound like my mom.

I spend a few hours alphabetizing Dad's albums (Abba to Frank Zappa). Having never outgrown my crayons, I decorate the cardboard boxes and shove them against the wall, creating a lovely makeshift casing for the records.

The final touch is Fu-Fu, whom I situate at the foot of my bed. It's possible I've had her in the wrong place all along. Perhaps this is why I have not reaped my fortune.

Kirby, Nina, and I are to meet at the corner of my street Monday morning for the first day of our U.S. History summer school class. We live in an isosceles triangle from each other, Nina being the farthest point from Kirby and me. My street corner is central for walking to school.

Once I get close enough and out of the fog, I spot Nina and Kirby. They're sitting on the ground, leaning back to back against the stop sign. Two blue-headed misfits. Nina's hair is tied in two separate braids on each side of her head. She looks like a renegade Girl Scout.

Nina yowls a big yawn. "Hey, Nattie."

"Hi, you two." They get up from the ground.

Kirby rubs his eyes. "Tell us, Natalie, why are we spending six weeks of our summer vacation going to school from the godforsaken hour of seven-thirty a.m.?"

"Yeah," says Nina. "Do tell. I'm too tired to remember."

I gladly explain. "Next year the two of you will be kissing my feet in appreciation because you will have what is called a free period." I put my arms around them. "Translation: an entire school year to sleep in during your nonexistent first period. Plus, this is the only way to guarantee being in the same class together. It'll be fun."

"Fine." Nina jumps in place. "I'm pumped! Let's

go." She leads us down the sidewalk and toward Portola High.

Kirby says, "Well, you missed the new reality show, the one called *I Want My Dog Back*."

I wince. "Oh, how'd that go?"

"Mrs. McClure had to pry Bogart out of my mom's arms."

"What'd you do last night?" I ask Nina.

"You won't believe it," she answers.

The three of us crowd the sidewalk, Nina in the middle. "What is it?" Kirby asks impatiently.

"Settle down, spazmo," Nina says. "I was going to hang out with Laney and Maryann last night, right? So we meet at Maryann's and Laney says to me, 'I have a surprise.' "

"She had a zit?" I say jokingly.

"Ha." Nina continues. "We walk over to Juniper Street and she takes us to the door of this house that her mom is selling. Apparently, the house is empty."

Kirby raises his eyebrows. "Yeah? And she took her clothes off?"

"Let her talk, perv." I reach behind Nina and playfully nudge him. He zips his lips and we keep walking.

"So she knows the access code to that little box on the doorknob and is like, 'We can go inside.' "

"Did you go in?" I ask.

"I did," Nina says.

"What did you do in there?" Kirby asks.

"Hung out. Played hide-and-seek. It was kinda neat, like our very own clubhouse."

Kirby fixes his gaze on me. "And where were you, Natalie?"

"My mom's old roommate's son showed up on Saturday."

Nina stops and gives me a push on the shoulder. "And you didn't say anything! Talk. Talk!"

"Who's spazzing now?" Kirby says.

I roll my eyes. "His name is Carver and he's just a guy. A regular guy."

Nina wags her finger. "No, we don't categorize people that way. A guy fits into one of two categories: you're interested or you're not."

"I disagree," says Kirby. Apparently, he's ready to jump into the discussion.

Nina turns to him. "Let it go. I'm talking to Natalie here." She can always get him to back down.

I think about it for a second. These are my two closest friends. Part of me wants to spill, but this is too complicated. Admitting any interest in Carver would only acknowledge that I'm attracted to him. Already I have a nymphlike creature performing acrobatics inside my stomach and doodling "Carver" on the lining of my aortic valve. Still, I'm trying not to like him, and I don't need Nina as part of the pro-Carver campaign. She'll only convince me of how great he is if I tell her I'm even remotely interested. "Not interested."

"Bummer!" Nina stomps her foot. "I totally pictured the two of you hitting it off. How great would it be to have the guy you like living on the premises?" Glad I didn't mention I was interested. We resume walking.

When we walk into the half-full classroom, Laney is at a desk in the back, with Maryann sitting beside her. I guess they want a free period next year, too, unfortunately.

They wave at Nina, motioning to a desk they've saved for her. With grace, she points to Kirby and me, a sign that we have her for at least the next few hours.

There are a few recognizable incoming seniors, who are obviously retaking the class. Then there're Richard Belstone and Christopher Dowling, who are seated in the front row, looking ready to expand their minds.

Nina and Kirby sit next to each other. I sit behind Nina.

In a few minutes, the classroom has filled. An elderly man walks through the door, looking like what one might find next to the word "codger" in an illustrated dictionary. He walks to the front of the classroom dressed in navy blue dress pants and a white short-sleeved button-up shirt.

The eye-catching piece of his wardrobe is a pair of

red, white, and blue suspenders that look as if they are truly the only things holding up his pants. He holds no briefcase, no coffee cup.

He turns to the white board and writes "Mr. Klinefelter." The stool he drags out from behind the podium scrapes along the dull linoleum floor. Positioned front and center, he sits on the edge of it, his white socks peeking out from his polished black dress shoes. " 'We hold these truths to be self-evident, that all men are created equal, that they are endowed by their Creator with certain unalienable Rights, that among these are Life, Liberty, and the pursuit of Happiness.' Anyone?"

Richard Belstone's hand thrusts up into the air. Mr. Klinefelter gives him a nod. "The Declaration of Independence, July 4, 1776."

Mr. Klinefelter juts his thumb forward. "You are correct, young man. Now, why might our declaration set us apart from other nations?"

Someone taps my shoulder. I turn around. The sleepy, sheep houndish–looking guy behind me holds out a folded piece of paper, a note. I take it and hide it in my hands under the desk.

Richard and Christopher raise their hands to answer the teacher's question. "Rhetorical, boys. Rhetorical. Think about this one."

I lean back in my seat, unfolding the note beneath the desktop. "Who is that guy in your upstairs room?" She doesn't have to sign it.

It's from Laney. Poor thing didn't have my cell number to text me, so she had to resort to pencil and paper.

"Freedom!" Mr. Klinefelter shouts, answering his own question. He slides off the stool and walks over to the window.

I'm not going to write back. I'm decidedly not thrilled about Carver living in my room, but I have the "freedom!" to keep him a secret.

At work, Carver gets to leave early. About two hours later, as Mom and I drive home together, we turn the corner onto our street and I see two silhouettes standing under the globe of the streetlight at the end of the cul-de-sac. As we get closer, it's clear, true— self-evident even—that Laney is in pursuit of happiness. She has found my secret.

Digging is a dog's effort to fill a void.

—Michael Kaplan, *The Manifesto of Dog*

Pip, Southpaw, and Otto have been trained to release any object in their mouth, be it bone, ball, or tennis shoe, when we say "Drop!" I want to shout "Drop!" to Laney right now because she's got Carver pinned underneath the streetlight in that metaphorical jaw of hers.

Mom and I step out of the car. I can hear the phone ringing and the dogs barking inside the house. I sprint past Mom up the walkway, unlock the door, and clamor to grab the phone in the kitchen. The dog entourage swarms and hobbles behind me.

"Hello?" I hurry to the living room, phone in hand, turn out the light, and peep through the slats in the wood shutters to get a clear view of Laney and Carver in the street.

"You turned off your cell again." It's Kirby.

"I was at work."

"You are not going to believe this."

Outside, Laney tosses her hair. Carver shifts his weight to the right. "Can I call you later, Kirby?"

"The dog is back."

"What?" I'm having a hard time paying attention to him. With a thin, graceful hand, Laney points down the street, toward town.

Kirby says, "Bogart. He was scratching at my front door when I came home." Laney and Carver start walking down the street, away from the cul-de-sac.

"I can't believe it!" I really wish I was referring to Bogart.

"I know, I know, it's nuts. The dog found his way back to us."

"Actually, bassets tend to wander and can easily backtrack. But you'll never guess who I'm watching out my window right now. She's walking down the street with Carver, swaying her hips like she's going to strip off her clothes and rub against him. Just guess who it is."

"Your grandma?" Kirby says.

"Ha-ha. Very funny. It's Laney. Where do you think they're going?"

"Why do you care? You said you weren't interested in him."

Carver and Laney are no longer in sight. Instead of running out the door to follow them, I sink into the couch. "It's just Laney, you know? Is there any guy she hasn't pounced on?"

"Ruh-huh," Kirby says in his best Scooby Doo voice.

"Kirb, you are way too brilliant and intimidating. She knows you'd reject her."

"Truer words have never been spoken."

I roll my eyes. "Well, I'm glad you and Bogart are reunited."

"Yeah, he's right here, on my lap. Want to say hi?"

I stand up from the couch, finding my own dogs perched next to their bowls. "Can't. Got to feed my own. Send him my love, though."

At ten-thirty p.m., I'm in my darkened bedroom, tucked under my covers and wearing earmuff-style headphones that are plugged into the stereo receiver. The record on the turntable spins. I'm listening to Billy Bragg thump the strings on his guitar in "The Myth of Trust," wishing that Carver could be a guitar-playing exchange student with a thick British accent and anti-Laney sentiment.

It was ingenious of me to move my bed, because I am looking out my window and can see Carver walk up the stairway to the room above the garage. With Laney.

I have taken what's important to me out of the room, but somehow I still feel violated when Carver opens the door for Laney and she walks inside.

Before he goes into the room behind her, he stands on the landing and turns to look directly into my window. I pull my covers up to my chin. I'm pretty sure he can't see me; he's too far away and my room is too dark.

Lucky for me, the belly of the moon is full of milky light, which generously pours down on Carver, allowing me to watch him.

Neutering reduces activity levels in male dogs, not bitches. —Michael Kaplan, *The Manifesto of Dog*

According to my digital clock, Laney was up in Carver's room last night from 10:31 to 10:37 p.m. I don't think six minutes is long enough for any substantial interaction (meaning a game of chess or steamy sex), but given my modest experience with guys, I can't speak with authority on the subject.

Today in history class, Mr. Klinefelter has dumped salt in my wound by putting together "cooperative groups." We will be meeting in these four-person groups daily. *Daily.*

After three minutes with my "cooperative group," I have decided that "cooperative group" now replaces "jumbo shrimp" as the most blatant oxymoron ever.

I am sitting here in my cooperative group and

there is one uncooperative component: Laney. Laney is in my group, which must mean that Mr. Klinefelter dislikes me very much and wants to make my life more miserable.

From afar I can handle Laney, but up close she makes me nervous. Unsettled. When I'm near her, I get the same feeling that I experience when I have to give a speech in front of a classroom full of people. I think it's fear.

Also in my group: Richard "Ivy League" Belstone and Allison "I'd Rather Be Anywhere Than Here" Meyer.

Poor Maryann. She sits in her group across the room, looking like she's shriveling, having been severed from her master, Laney.

Mr. Klinefelter has asked our cooperative groups to look through some newspapers and form an opinion about whether biased reporting manipulates the public and thus abuses the First Amendment.

Naturally, Richard assumes the group-leader role. "Okay, Laney, you look through the *Wall Street Journal*. Natalie, you get the *New York Times*, and, Allison, here's the *Christian Science Monitor*."

Allison scowls at Richard, narrowing her charcoal black–rimmed eyes. "I'm an atheist."

Richard takes a pencil from behind his ear and points it at Allison. "It's not a religious publication. The CIA reads the *Christian Science Monitor* because—"

Allison interrupts with a grunt and says, "Trade me." Richard hands over his copy of the *Washington Post*.

I become my own group behind my fully unfolded newspaper until Laney moves it aside like a curtain.

"I met Carver," she says brazenly. My heart starts beating faster.

I'm able to mutter only a one-syllable word: "Good."

"Is something wrong? Are you mad at him?" She says this forcefully, like she's accusing me of something.

"No." I swallow hard and feel myself dissolve into my desk. Laney is sitting down, but I sense her circling me, prowling. She is the devil dog Spitz incarnate from Jack London's *Call of the Wild*—my all-time favorite book. Like Spitz, Laney provokes, snarls, and prepares to bite.

"Hmm," she says, nodding. "We were hanging out in his room last night." She pauses for emphasis. I want to tell her that spending six minutes in someone's room does not qualify as "hanging out." That's just "dropping in."

She continues. "He said you seem like you're mad at him." Hair toss. "I told him that's just how you are." Ouch! There's the bite.

"Oh," I say, stunned. Having slammed me down to size, Laney refocuses on her *Wall Street Journal*.

I fan the newspaper back into barrier position, but

now it's limp and crumpled because Laney poked at it.

I hate that Laney and Carver had a conversation about me. In my room. I try to distract myself with an article on the all-time-low national deficit, but all I can think about is Laney and Carver. Carver and Laney. Laner and Carvey. I wish I could spit words back into Laney's face the way she does to me.

I'm no stranger to the scenario of the meek kid on the playground getting bullied by the powerful, more popular kid. Oftentimes in my past I have been that meek kid. The one who in elementary school gave up her place in the lunch line to avoid the tyranny of ponytailed Hannah Hopkins. Without protest, I let Hailey Lansky have my favorite Washington Monument light-up pen that Dad had brought back from his tour in Washington, D.C., only because I was too scared to ask for it back. And just last year, I had to take a zero on a math homework assignment because Maddy Fletcher borrowed my work during lunch and broke her promise to return it to me before sixth period. I never said anything to Maddy about it.

It's people like me who keep the high and mighty positioned on their thrones. Coward!

For the remainder of class, my stomach growls with fury. Carver and Laney discussed me. Behind my back. This only fuels my anti-Carver fire.

Having no other outlet for my anger, I practically

storm home after school, alone. I do not linger at the vending machine with Nina and Kirby after class. I do not get in Laney's face and tell her to shove the red licorice she's eating up her butt. I do not pass Go and collect two hundred dollars.

What I'm about to do is in the spirit of self-preservation. I haven't started filling my two-lie quota for the summer season, so it is okay that I am going to bear down and start hatching one.

When I get home, I call Mom at the clinic. Carver answers the phone. What could've happened between yesterday and today that got him promoted from cleaning crew to receptionist, I'm not sure. I pause after he answers as I consider saying something to him like "Please, don't talk about me to Laney Benning, you insensitive jerk," but instead I muffle my voice and ask for Dr. Kaplan, hoping he doesn't recognize me. I don't think he does.

Mom comes to the phone and I give birth to my lie. I tell her I came directly home from school because I feel sick. Mom wants details and I give them ("I ate a carton of expired yogurt"), but I don't get immunity from having to go to work until I use the magic word: diarrhea. Once I say it, she tells me to rest and drink plenty of water. Phew.

I climb into bed with my U.S. History textbook. Pip, Southpaw, and Otto join me. My dark blue comforter is due for a wash; it looks like the pelt of a wild animal from all the shedded dog hair. But I refuse to do laundry today. A day off is in order, even if I have to crouch behind a lie about having loose stools.

Grandma takes too many trips up the stairs to check on me and insists that I drink chamomile tea. She also gives me my mail: a new issue of *The Bark* magazine, with William Wegman's signature silver Weimaraners on the cover, and a postcard from Dad, who's in England.

On one side of the postcard is Tower Bridge, which I assume is the bridge that is falling down, or did fall down. I'm not sure. The bridge in the picture looks structurally sound, so they must have fixed it. On the other side of the card is Dad's rushed scrawl.

> Dear Natalie,
>   Spent the week with the Siberian Husky Club of Great Britain. Getting ready for Germany. I'll e-mail you my itinerary in the next few days. I look forward to seeing you in August when I'm home in L.A. I'll call soon.
>   Love and, as they say here, cheers!
>   Dad

Dad has always held an adoration for the wolflike Siberian husky. Huskies are a breed with exceptional stamina, but they also have an innate urge to roam.

81

And here I am in my bed with my fake diarrhea, wondering if everything I've ever learned about lying came from Dad's love for a breed of dog that has a natural tendency to stray.

I place his postcard in the shoe box under my bed, one of many containing letters, cards, and printed e-mails from Dad. Though I hardly see him, there's a paper trail of him under my bed. Better than nothing.

For the next few hours, I nap, read *The Bark* cover to cover, and start listening with my headphones to Dad's Stevie Wonder albums in chronological order, from *Talking Book* to *Songs in the Key of Life*. I wish I could be in the room above the garage. There is more sunlight up there, more space than in my elfin bedroom.

Carver's already abused the area by inviting Laney inside. I bet the room will suffer more punishment from his poor judgment. He's probably got a fish tank up there already. And maybe even a cat.

By the time I get to *Innervisions*, the second Stevie Wonder album in Dad's collection, I have decided, for the integrity of the room above the garage, that it is my obligation to see how Carver is choosing to inhabit it. He is like a new puppy, and if left unattended, puppies will chew on furniture and piddle on the floor.

I lurch out of bed, stub my toe on Fu-Fu—youch!—and pull the needle from the record. The dogs stay bunked on the mattress as if they, too, are feigning the runs. I give each of them a well-deserved rub on the tummy.

Carver is at work. Grandma checked in about five minutes ago and is downstairs making chicken soup. I tiptoe down the stairway, out the front door, and up the steps leading to the room above the garage.

A dog's hyperactivity is a symptom, not a character trait. —Michael Kaplan, *The Manifesto of Dog*

I've determined that if the door to the room above the garage is unlocked, I have every right to go inside. That would show that Carver is careless about his possessions and has little regard for privacy. But if the door is locked, I will take this as a sign from the universe that I shouldn't go inside, and I will return to the Stevie Wonder marathon in my room.

The doorknob gives when I twist it. Once inside, I shut the door behind me. I am so familiar with the room that it takes no more than a few seconds to notice what's different about it.

Carver has mounted a disco ball on the ceiling.

Bold move.

I would have had to fill out extensive paperwork with my mom to plug in a dinky night-light up here.

Did he get her permission? Probably not. I'm instantly envious of his bravery, and if I weren't trying so hard to dislike him, I might put his courage into the same category as the remarkably enduring Eskimo dog's.

The room looks tidy: the futon is in a couch position, a comforter on top tucked neatly into a puffy square. An open laptop computer lies on the futon, a generic Microsoft screen saver bouncing across the monitor. There's a small pile of clothes in one corner. The rest are folded in Carver's duffel bags.

There are no signs of Laney, no pair of pink underwear on the ground, no snapshot of Carver and Laney holding hands on the beach at sunset.

I've seen only one other boy-room in my life: Kirby's. His is plastered with Beatles posters and carpeted with unwashed clothes, and it stinks like dirty socks. The Carver-inhabited room smells different. It's a good smell, a savory smell, like one of Grandma's basil plants in her herb garden. He's left the windows open, and the salty coastal afternoon breeze has made its way inside.

I walk over to the futon and look at the pictures that Carver has taped to the wall next to it.

The first set of 4×6 photographs are of koi, some orange, some white mottled with black. They are scaly, whiskered, and aerodynamic-looking, but I'm just not impressed.

Next picture on the wall: a close-up of a huge dragonfly perched on the trumpet of a bright pink flower bloom. I stare at the intricate circuit of veins splayed on each of its four transparent wings. Definitely more impressive than the fish, that's for sure.

The only picture with people in it is what looks like a recent photo of Carver and his mom at graduation. He wears a black cap and gown. A white tassel dangling from his mortarboard almost covers one of his green eyes. His arm is gently wrapped around his mom's shoulders. They look happy with each other, their smiles sincere.

There's a picture missing from the wall. I can tell because there's tape where it should be. I glance down at my feet and spot the photo on the floor. When I pick it up to take a look, a crop of goose bumps perks up along my arms.

The picture is of a wet black Labrador retriever standing on the borderline between sand and ocean. It's a side view of the dog looking out at the sea. He is a gorgeous dog, robust and broad-headed. He wears a red bandanna around his neck and holds a piece of driftwood in his mouth. This may be the dog Carver lost recently. A pang of guilt stabs at me for not having asked him about the details. The thought of Laney being up here wipes it away.

However, I do line up the corners of the picture with the tape on the wall, pressing it until it sticks. I sit down on the futon to take another look and accidentally land on the keyboard of Carver's laptop. Turning around, I see I've knocked it out of sleep mode. And there's an open e-mail on the screen.

I read it, even though it's none of my business. It's there, and I can't seem to help myself. The subject: MISS YOU.

There's a girlfriend in the mix?

Eyes scan down to the sender: his mom.

Relief.

The e-mail:

Hi Carv,

Sorry I missed your call earlier today. Glad to hear you are settling in.

Miss you. Miss our morning talks.

Love you to the moon and back, chum.

Mom

My mouth curls into a smile. The pixie in my stomach sighs when I reread the words "miss our morning talks" and "chum."

Then footsteps, more than one set, clomp up the stairs.

Carver is supposed to be at work! He can't walk in and see me here!

I dash to the closet, because I would rather be a missing person living in darkness and subsisting on a diet of spiders and mothballs than have anyone find me poking around the room like some freak-o stalker.

Knocking. "Carver? Are you home?" Laney.

"Carvey?" Maryann now. Carvey? Ick.

Waiting. Leave. Please leave. Waiting.

Clomp. Clomp. Clomp. They are leaving.

After counting to one hundred, I crawl out of the closet and over to the window. Slowly, I raise my head until one eye can periscope onto Laney's porch, where she is now walking up the steps with Maryann. They disappear into her house. I sprint to the door and retreat into my own.

Later in the afternoon, Grandma brings a tray with a bowl of chicken broth up to my room, which means I don't have to face Carver at the dinner table.

Mom checks on me when she gets home, feels my forehead, rubs my back. And my stomach starts to hurt for real because I am exploiting the affection of my own mother. But it feels good to have her here. The attention is nice, soothing, and, unfortunately, fleeting.

The next day at school, the prospect of cooperative group is harrowing, but I live through it by focusing on George Washington's farewell speech of 1796 instead of dealing with Laney Benning's demonic stare of the twenty-first century.

After school, Nina, Kirby, and I walk into town together. We agree to meet at Miguel's at six p.m. for our weekly soup night. Half-price soup. Mom only recently began allowing me this pleasure, because walking with friends into town is acceptable at sixteen, no sooner. I think she's okay with soup night because it is a controlled environment, and she can always "pop in" should she see fit. She'll call me at some point in the evening anyway. The woman needs a Valium, I swear.

Nina and Kirby break off at the wishbone on Highway 101 that leads to Rescued Threads, while I walk toward work with apprehension at my heels.

When I walk into the reception area, there is a very sick saluki hound shivering under her creamy coat. She doesn't bother to lift her long narrow muzzle from the ground.

"Hi," I say to her owner, a pretty forty-something woman whose sharp eyebrows are sloped in concern. "Can I get you something?"

"No, thanks," she replies.

"Not feeling well, huh?" I bend down to the dog. "What's her name?" I ask.

"Emira."

I reach out my hand for Emira to sniff. She doesn't move, but she lets me stroke her long silky ear. "We'll get you all better, girl."

I walk over to the reception desk. My body jolts slightly when I notice Carver sitting behind it.

It was wise of me to stay home yesterday. I didn't have to wrestle the fairy dust out of Pixie's hand in order to keep it together. I am out of control! Why do my insides go into spasms when I see this guy?

Logically, I should be miffed at Carver. He and Laney Benning talked about me behind my back. (But I did sneak up to his room and learn that his mother calls him chum.)

Carver gets out of the chair. The caramel-colored hairs on his forearms gleam in the terrible fluorescent light.

"Your mom had me man the desk this morning. Here," he says, motioning to the chair. "Have a seat. I think you do this much better than I do. I had to press about twenty buttons on the phone before I found the right one to make an outgoing phone call." Phone call? Outgoing? Work-related? Laney-related? Mom discourages phone calls that are not work-related.

I set my backpack down on the floor underneath the desk and take a seat in the chair. It's still warm from Carver.

He goes to the back, reappears with a plastic cup filled with water, and hands it to Emira's owner. Then he reaches inside the storage room, fetches the broom, and sweeps. Mom hasn't given him free roam of the kennel run yet. The clinic floor has never been so clean.

"Are you feeling better?" Carver asks me as he sweeps the corner nearest the reception desk.

I'm hit with a crippling thought: I'm almost positive that Carver ate dinner with Mom and Grandma last night. Inevitably, the conversation must have spent some time hovering around my well-being, in which case Grandma probably gave Mom an update. I have no doubt Grandma used the word "diarrhea." In a German accent, no less. Grandmas do these sorts of things. Just last night, she asked me point-blank if I'd had a hard "bowel movement" yet. Gross.

The idea of Carver looking at me with the D word levitating over his head is embarrassing enough to make a constellation of sweat beads form on my upper lip.

"Um, yeah." I nod. "Feeling better."

"Good." Carver shuffles to another corner. The muscles in his arms expand and contract as he shifts the broom back and forth.

After Emira is in the exam room, I escape to the kennel run to commune with the dogs.

Later in the afternoon, when Mom has a cancellation, she's catching up on paperwork in her office. I knock on her open door.

She looks over her glasses and waves me in.

"Tonight is soup night. Just wanted to make sure it's okay if I go."

"How's your stomach?" Mom asks again, for the fourth time in an hour.

"Better."

"I don't think it's a good idea. Yesterday at this time, you were curled up in your bed with a stomachache." She must not have spying hardware hooked up in my room yet, because I wasn't exactly curled up in my bed all afternoon.

"Really, I'm feeling a lot better," I say.

Mom looks at me and bites her lip. "Make sure you stick with something bland tonight. Stay away from the salsa." Wait, is she actually starting to trust me? She knows how much I love salsa.

Mom scratches her nose. I get up to leave. "Be home by nine. Do you have your phone?" she asks.

I pull my phone from my pocket. Mom is big on proof.

"Love you," she says.

But I feel cheated, because it's not to the moon and back.

14

Dogs are influenced by stimuli, not morality.

—Michael Kaplan, *The Manifesto of Dog*

On Friday, during an overview of the 1791 Bill of Rights, Allison Meyer informs our cooperative group that Spud Garcia is having a party tonight. There will be a keg. His parents are "out of town."

I'm right on top of the "out of town" thing. I decided a long time ago that "out of town" is a tropical resort where parents from all over the world congregate so that the kids who have been left behind can do things like throw parties in the parents' absence. Wherever this "out of town" place may be, my mom has yet to go there, and I doubt she ever will.

It is quite puzzling that Allison would bother to tell us about Spud's party. The entire week she has done nothing but scowl at us.

Allison gives us the details, then Laney looks at me. "Are you going?" Her voice holds the tone typically used with the question "Did you fart?" I shrug.

Although I am unable to respond verbally to Laney's question, my newfound aspiration in life is to attend Spud's party. I have been to a few parties in high school, including Maryann's nightmare slumber party, but they were small-scale, more like get-togethers involving Cranium and twelve-packs of beer (or bottled wine). But this is a "kegger," which translates as "big epic party."

This is my opportunity for personal growth.

While Nina uses the rest room after class, Kirby and I wait nearby on a bench and eat CornNuts.

"We're going to Spud Garcia's party tonight," I tell Kirby.

News of a party travels at lightning speed, because Kirby already knows about it. "Do you think..." He clears his throat. "Do you think they'll be doing what they did at Maryann's slumber party?"

I pause, my tongue absorbing the salt from a CornNut. "Who doing what?" I ask.

"You know." Kirby widens his brown eyes. His glasses shift upward. He wiggles his chest.

"That's why you want to go? You think girls are going to be showing their boobs?"

Kirby shifts a bit. "Course not." He looks at his feet with a thin smile.

"Pig."

"I'm kidding. C'mon." He elbows me in the side and pours more CornNuts into the cup of his hand. "Is Cramer going tonight?"

"Carver."

"Yeah, whatever."

"Why do you care?"

"It's been a week, Natalie. We haven't met him yet. I think you made him up. He's your new imaginary friend, isn't he?"

I hold up my hands in surrender. "Got me!"

"So you think your mom is going to let you go tonight?" Kirby asks.

"No, but I'm pretty sure she'll let me hang out at Nina's house," I say with a wink.

Mom assumes that I'll be at Nina's house and that Kirby will take me home after I call her to tell her we're on our way.

The real plan is to meet at the corner around eight p.m., after I return from taking Grandma to rummy. Nina, Kirby, and I are going to walk to Spud's together; that way if any one of us decides to get blitzed (highly unlikely), we won't have to drive. I won't be staying long, since I have a curfew of ten p.m., but at least I get an extra hour, because I told Mom we were watching a movie at Nina's. If I had to be home at nine, I wouldn't be able to see the entire movie. Mom herself always says I should finish what I start.

I have spent my two summer lies in the first week of summer, a sort of lying spree. The severity of my imminent wrongdoing is lessened in my mind as I remind myself that I have been a model child. I deserve to go to this party. I've earned it. And I am merely protecting Mom from having to worry about me.

Spud Garcia has been a varsity linebacker since our freshman year. He is built like a potato but has the brains of a mathematician. Spud's smarts justify the football players' need to wear helmets. I've been in classes with him. We know each other, but I don't think we've ever had a conversation.

When we arrive at the party, Nina rings the doorbell. "I heard that Spud's mom collects doll heads," she says. "Later we gotta find where she keeps them."

"Oh, so that's why you're here," says Kirby. "I thought it was for the beer, but you're really after doll heads."

"Of course." Nina smirks. "You don't think I'm that shallow, do you? Doll heads over beer any day, my friend."

Spud answers the door with a plastic cup domed in froth. "Hey, come on in," he says. One would think he's curling a heavy dumbbell instead of a beer the way his bicep bulges from his T-shirt sleeve. It looks like a miniature head of a rottweiler.

Inside the house, it's nothing like the keggers I've

seen in movies. No one is hooting or hollering. There are no bras or boxer shorts dangling from the chandelier in the entryway. No one has driven a car or a motorcycle through the large front window facing the street. But we are early. I guess there's still time.

Ushered through French doors, we congregate by the keg in the backyard. Jake Chapman is serving the guests with the keg nozzle and hands Nina a full cup of beer. He must think I'm waiting for one, too, because he squirts beer into an empty cup and passes it to me. I take it. Kirby gives me a look and accepts the next one Jake offers. Neither one of us slurps a sip, regardless of Nina's swallowing hers with effortless gulps.

Nina is comfortable in any element. She's probably not thinking of the possibility of the party being broken up by the cops or the fact that Spud's parents are out of town and he's throwing this party without their permission.

There're about twenty people here so far. People are talking and sipping, but who's to say anyone, besides Nina and the handful of people chugging around the keg, is actually drinking? I could be one of many who merely hold their cups, hoping to blend into the party.

Just as I resolve to take a small sip of the beer in my hand, my phone starts barking. I place my beer on the barbecue lid, run inside to the nearest room, and shut the door behind me. "Hello?" I'm in what looks like a guest room.

"Natalie?" Mom. "Did you give Southpaw her diethylstilbestrol?"

"Yes," I answer, hoping that Mom is calling out of a genuine concern for Southpaw's incontinence and not in an attempt to keep tabs on me.

"Okay, then. Are you having a good time?"

"Yeah, we're just watching the movie."

"What movie?" Is she kidding?

"Shaun of the Dead." It was the last movie I saw, still fresh in my mind should Mom ask about plot points.

"Well, have fun," she says. "I'll see you at ten, no later. Call before you leave."

"Bye, Mom." We hang up. I think of my beer sitting out on the barbecue. I thought I'd take some sips, but now I don't think it's worth it. Any hint of beer on my breath would have Mom on the phone finding a rehab facility for me.

I try to resist it, but I feel kind of sorry for Mom. It's Friday night and she's worried about the dog not getting her incontinence medicine. That's just not right.

Forty-five minutes later, about fifty more people have arrived at Spud's. I've yet to see Allison Meyer, and I'm getting worried that at some point Spud's neighbors will call the cops because of the noise.

Kirby and I sit in the kitchen, our beers untouched but still gripped in our hands. Nina is mostly out back socializing but checks in with us from time to time. It's nice of her, but I'd rather have her full attention.

Kirby and I have just witnessed two guys eat a dozen raw eggs. I watch yolk trickle down the chin of egg eater number one. "Well, I'm ready to go."

I set my cup on the granite countertop, but I reconsider and pick it back up. I've been trained not to leave a mess.

"Let's go, then," Kirby says before raising his cup, licking his lips, dipping his head down, and pretending to take a huge slurp.

"Ooh, that was a good one!" I say. "You win." We've been fake drinking for the duration of the party. His performance has been quite theatrical, peppered with burps and glugging sound effects.

"I'm gonna use the rest room first." Kirby walks away, cup in hand. Good timing, because the two egg guys reopen the refrigerator and pull out a bottle of Tabasco sauce.

I head toward the backyard to say good-bye to Nina, but Laney and Maryann have arrived. They create a force field around Nina with their matching flowy short-short pink skirts and tight cleavage-revealing tank tops. From their cups they swig beer and it looks as though they are really drinking, because the three of them are leaning on each other lazily.

I don't have the strength to face Laney right now, so I give a hearty good-bye wave to Nina from afar. She makes a phone-to-ear gesture.

I trace my footsteps back into the house and walk down one of two hallways. Hallway one is where Kirby stands at the end of a long line for the bathroom. On the other side is hallway two, empty as a wind tunnel.

Next to me, at the front end of the hallway, is an ivy plant, its vines climbing from a large terra-cotta planter. Making sure I don't have anyone's attention, I pour my beer into the dark soil of the planter. I hope alcohol is not lethal to ivy.

Then I remember something. Instead of going to hallway one and standing in line with Kirby, I search down hallway two for the magic door that might lead to the mystic heads of dolls.

I go to the door farthest down the hallway. It is the only one that is shut. I press my ear to the door and knock lightly. No one answers; no one is grunting. It's safe.

An entire wall of doll heads, neatly encased in a huge glass shelving unit, watch me as I walk into the room. Recessed lighting inside the case illuminates the collection. There are rows and rows of them, some porcelain, some plastic, some as small as grapes, others as big and smooth as honeydew melons. Not one has a neck.

"That has got to be the freakiest thing I've ever

seen." I turn around. Carver stands about five feet away from me.

Pixie breaks out and starts doing cancan kicks in my stomach. She does this so quickly, I don't even have time to stop her.

Potty training should be executed with diligence and discipline. —Michael Kaplan, *The Manifesto of Dog*

If you rent a hotel room for a newlywed poodle and Labrador retriever and let them consummate their marriage, a couple of months later you'll have yourself a litter of labradoodles. Do the same with a cocker spaniel and a poodle: the result is an adorable brood of cockapoos.

Carver and I are alone in this room (among ogling doll heads), but honestly, I'm not sure what the result is going to be. All I know is that I feel like a mutt, a mixed breed of fear and excitement.

Carver says, "I thought you were at your friend's house tonight." Did he ask Mom about my Friday-night plans?

"Yeah, well, I don't know about your mom, but I

couldn't tell mine I was going to a kegger." I'm squeezing my cup to the point of strangling it.

"On my honor," he says, lifting up his hand, "I will not tell your mom I saw you here."

He looks so good. He's wearing a dark green T-shirt under a plaid flannel button-up shirt. The earthy colors lure the green from his eyes. His jeans hang on him just right, sagging not so much that his boxer shorts are showing, but enough that if I were to pull up his T-shirt, I'd spy a belly button. A pair of Birkenstock sandals expose his bubbly toes; the big one on his right foot is wrapped in a turban of gauze.

Carver notices me staring at his foot. "Mammoth splinter. Piece of wood jutting out from the stairs on the side of the garage." I shift my focus back to the doll heads. Carver walks over to stand next to me. "Your grandma took it out."

I can't believe this, but I giggle. "Did she use her dagger?"

Carver laughs. "She had me prop my foot up on the couch and came back from the kitchen with this huge knife. I swear I thought she was going to cut off my toe."

"Sounds about right. She's a big believer in the knife versus the tweezers. Claims there's less infection."

"I didn't know such a controversy existed," says Carver. He takes a sip of his beer and points to a tangerine-sized doll head. It is the color of an eggshell, with pink cheeks, pale blue eyes, and a huge crack down its center. "How old do you think that is?"

I remember something important: no doubt Carver came here with Laney. "I'd better go," I say, and start to walk toward the door.

"Hold up a minute," Carver says. I stop in my tracks. "Is something wrong? I mean, have I said anything in the past week to offend you, something that put you off?"

I squeak out a no.

"Are you mad about me feeding your dog chocolate? In my defense, I was only nine and had no idea chocolate could kill a dog. I'm really sorry about that."

I turn toward him. "He got really sick, you know."

"But he was okay, right?" Carver asks. "Boys do stupid things sometimes. I was only trying to impress you."

"By giving my dog chocolate?"

Carver takes a step closer to me. "You seemed to really like that dog. I thought if he liked me, you'd like me, too. So I kept feeding him stuff."

"That's why he followed you everywhere."

"Yeah, but when I gave him the chocolate, my plan kind of backfired."

Carver was trying to impress me.

I am beginning to feel heat pressing against my

entire body. My head is competing with my heart for airtime. I take a deep breath. "I gotta go. I have to be home by ten tonight."

"I'll walk with you," he offers. "I'm not much for parties. Laney said you weren't that into the social scene, either." He looks straight at me when he says this.

I can go from zero to one hundred with this guy.

Here it comes. I'm going to say it. "I should explain, since you haven't noticed, that Laney and I aren't close." I'm using the same voice Dad uses with dogs during training sessions, low and firm. "Although I am not used to being around *her* kind of people, I am quite comfortable being around normal people." The doll heads look as surprised as I am; I've just told Carver what I think. "It'd be nice if you two didn't talk about me behind my back."

"Sorry about that. Laney mentioned you without me asking. All I'm trying to say is that I've been here at this party for about"—he looks at his watch—"ten minutes, and I'm ready to leave. I could walk home with you. We are going to the same place." He casually steps past me and heads out the door of doll-head room.

"Didn't you come here with Laney?" I ask. Now he stops in his tracks, turns, and comes back into the room. "Shouldn't you leave with her?" Why would Carver ditch Laney and her cantaloupes to walk home with me?

"Yes, I came here with Laney. No, I don't need to leave with her. She's cool, but we're just friends."

That wasn't what I meant, yet it's nice to have the extra information.

Kirby will be annoyed if Carver walks home with us, I'm sure of it. I know him too well. He doesn't like a change in plans. And what if Kirby sees through me and notices my perspiring profusely from the Carver-induced rise of my body heat?

"It's okay. I'll just see you tomorrow." Pixie elbows me right in the ribs, probably because she thinks I'm crazy to leave here without him.

"All right, I'll see you tomorrow," he says. "I'm just going to keep looking at the heads. Maybe if I look at them long enough, they'll come to life." He makes a *poof!* gesture with his free hand and moves closer to the hundred pairs of lucky doll-head eyes.

I meet Kirby in the hallway. "What did you do?" he asks.

"What do you mean?"

He leans over and points into my empty cup. He lowers his voice. "You pounded your beer, didn't you?"

I point to the ivy plant. I whisper, "I poured it in there when no one was looking."

Kirby smirks. "I poured all of mine in the toilet. But the planter . . . That's brilliant."

Yeah, brilliant. I want to be back in the doll-head room with Carver, feeling the ping and drip of feverish giddiness warming my insides. Carver, who apologized for feeding Troy chocolate. Carver, who tried to impress me. Carver, who doesn't like parties, either. Carver, who'd rather walk home with me than stay at a party with a keg and Laney Benning.

16

Biting is a cry for help from a spiritually wounded dog.

—Michael Kaplan, *The Manifesto of Dog*

In the reception area at work the next morning, Vernon passes out our Saturday warm beverages.

Mom sips her Earl Grey tea. "Carver, you've been here over a week. You're ready to meet the dogs." She says it like a proclamation, as if Carver is graduating from doggie boot camp. Mom is right about one thing: meeting the dogs is a privilege.

I assume that Mom or Vernon will lead Carver through Dog Kennel for Beginners, but before I can get to the reception desk to squelch Pixie, Mom says, "Natalie, take Carver on back. I'll join you in a few minutes, after I return this phone call." Mom waves a pink message slip and heads toward her office.

"Let's head on back," says Carver, echoing Mom.

He's eager. And I don't blame him. Poor guy has been working with fish.

Deep breath. It was worth telling Carver how I felt last night because today I feel more at ease with him. "Follow me."

When we get to the mouth of the kennel, the dogs begin their barking ceremony. The earsplitting yelps and deep woofs rebound off the cement floor, up to the high ceiling, and into a blur of echoes. "Hold on a sec," I say loudly.

"Sure," Carver says over the noise. I step away, hoping Carver isn't looking at my butt right now, and walk the corridor of the kennel run, motioning with a flat hand so that the dogs know to bring it down. Dad taught me this trick.

From behind the chain-link gates of the individual kennels, I make eye contact with each dog, from furballed to shorthaired. The procession of barks thins as I reach the end.

I walk back to Carver, whose eyebrows arch at me.

"How did you do that?" he asks.

"What?" I hold my arms behind my back like I'm in some sort of restraint harness.

"They're quiet."

"Oh, well, they just wanted to know who was here. You should see my dad. I swear, one look from him and a dog just knows to stop barking." Each time I let my eyes hover on Carver for more than a second, Pixie does a one-handed cartwheel.

Get back to business. "So," I say, clapping my hands one time, kindergarten-teacher style.

"Are all the dogs here sick?" Carver asks.

"No, some just board here." We walk over to the first kennel, where Zenobia, an overfed keeshond with a magnificent coat of gray fur, is staying. Carver bends down in front of her kennel while she stretches her paw underneath her gate to him. "Wow," he says over a straggling bark at the end of the run, "what a beautiful dog."

Poetry doesn't have to rhyme. Sometimes it's hearing something you rarely say but often think. Carver sees beauty. In a dog. I might have had a hunch about this after seeing the picture of the black Lab up in his room, but it's now confirmed.

"Zenobia's owner is out of town a couple of times each month." I'm very aware of my breathing. Exhale. Inhale. "She's here on leisure. Go on in."

Carver gently unhooks her kennel gate. Zenobia huddles down playfully and keeps her ears back, a sign that Carver is welcome.

"I can see why you like it here," he says with a big smile. At first I'm not sure if he's talking to Zenobia or me. "There're no head games with dogs, you know? They either like you or they don't." Zenobia rolls onto her back, allowing Carver to rub her belly.

By the time we approach the last kennel of the run, I am more convinced that Carver may be able to rid himself of a life of fish and cross over to dogdom.

There has been no mention of cats and he has had something special to say about each dog: docile, affectionate, energetic, hyper, intelligent, outgoing, confident. He never used the same word twice.

I think he is forgiven for taking away my room. I really do.

Simon, a Doberman mix, stays curled in the corner of his space in the last kennel. His right paw is bandaged and is limply elevated over his left. Discharge goos in the inner corners of his eyes. "Simon here, he's a stray," I say. "I found him in the handball courts at school. I called Vernon to come and help me get him. Poor thing was shivering with fear. We had to coax him into the car with food."

Before I can stop him, Carver compassionately places a finger in the cage, and Simon lurches forward and nips Carver.

"Yow!" he screams, pulling his finger from the gate and tucking it into his other hand.

"Oh my God!" I shout. Simon folds back into his corner and the barking rises from the other dogs in their kennels. "Are you okay?"

Carver cups his bit finger in his hand as if he is holding a wounded mouse. "Yeah," he answers. "It's bleeding. And throbbing."

"We have to get you to a sink!" I grab his arm and lead him to the bathroom. As I run ahead of him, he staggers behind.

When we get to the sink, I immediately squirt

about a dozen small blobs of soap into my palm and motion Carver to bring his hand forward. His finger looks like it's been smeared with ketchup.

"Natalie?" Carver's voice is quivering a little.

"Uh-huh? Uh-huh?" I run the warm water over his finger and gently clean out his wound.

"Not to be mean or anything, but why are you so, uh, freaked out?"

My heart is pounding like an urgent fist on a door.

He's right. I am freaking out. "We've got to wash this wound out to make sure it's clear of Simon's saliva." I continue to scrub, adding soap and rolling his finger between my hands. "Have you had a tetanus shot recently?"

"Yes," he replies.

Hmmm. I wonder if he was bit by a fish. Do fish bite? "Did you step on a rusty nail or something?"

"No, I got a tattoo."

Tattoo?

"Why are you in a panic?" he asks.

"Well, he might have rabies. Simon is a stray, re-member?" Carver's face loses its mountain-climber glow. His cheeks are a shade of parsnip rather than cherry. Not good. I am nearing the end of a nervous breakdown and Carver's poor finger is at its epicenter.

Now I'm fixated on finding out where his tattoo is hiding. "I mean, he probably doesn't have rabies. In all the time I've worked here, a dog has never come in with rabies. It's just a good idea to wash the area for a solid fifteen minutes."

I've got to keep calm. Raccoons get rabies. Bats get rabies. Good-looking guys from Northern California do not get rabies. I keep washing, slowing down the pace a bit.

"So how do you know if a dog has rabies?" Carver asks warily.

"Well, you really have to do an autopsy on the brain to confirm it for sure."

"My brain?"

"No, the dog's brain. But the dog is quarantined for ten days and if he shows signs of rabies, like being scared of water or becoming really aggressive, he'll be put down. Then they'll do an autopsy on his brain. I'm sure you'll be okay, though."

"How do I know if I have rabies?"

"Same stuff. You'd be delirious. It takes anywhere from two days to two weeks to know, but Simon's been with us for"—I tally up the days in my head—"thirteen days, and he has shown no sign of rabies. His paw was infected; that's why he's bandaged up."

"Oh," he says. "So you don't think he has rabies?"

"Well, unless he gets strangely aggressive by tomorrow and starts trembling at the sight of his water bowl, I'd say you're safe."

"Does biting my finger count as strangely aggressive?"

There's a red dot on Simon's kennel tag, meaning

he has to be approached slowly. He needs time to smell the scent of someone, time to figure out what's next. I should have told Carver this, but his finger entered Simon's cage before I had a chance. "He's sort of sensitive," I explain.

"Phew," Carver sighs. The pink is coming back into the circles of his cheeks. "For a minute there, I was feeling a bit like Old Yeller."

My scrubbing comes to a pause. I look into those green eyes of his.

Carver referenced *Old Yeller*. He's notably more good-looking than he was two seconds ago. I resume cleansing, feeling the muscles in Carver's hand relax beneath the lather.

I totally get what he means when he says he feels like Old Yeller. (It was one of my favorite books as a kid, and I have seen the movie twenty-seven times.) Old Yeller got rabies while trying to protect his family from a wolf. And his young keeper, Travis, in a tear-jerking moment, is forced to kill him with a shotgun so that he won't suffer.

If Carver is Old Yeller, then I am definitely a female version of Travis. Unlike Travis's mom, mine isn't hollering over my shoulder, commanding me to shoot my Old Yeller. I might get to keep him. (At this point it should be noted that I *want* to keep him.)

I'm still washing his finger. Neither one of us is in a panic anymore. Suddenly, I realize that I might be washing his finger because it thrills me to touch him, so I pull my hands away.

"Sorry, I didn't mean to alarm you or anything. I have a tendency to jump to the worst-case scenario. I'll go get my mom so she can take a closer look." His eyes are warm, glinty. The tattoo on his body becomes a mystery that I must soon solve, even if I have to request politely that he remove articles of clothing so that I can break the case.

I walk out of the bathroom, toward my mom's office.

I'm excited about Carver and want to tell him that you have to earn a dog's trust before you reach out to him. It's not the bark. It's not the bite. It's the saliva and the stuff in it you can't really see that will always get you in the end.

A dog is most dangerous out of its element.

—Michael Kaplan, *The Manifesto of Dog*

That afternoon, Carver sweeps the empty reception area with his pointer finger mummified in gauze.

I steal glances at him from behind my desk. Mom was convinced Simon didn't have rabies, and coated Carver's finger in a shield of germicide before bandaging it. She also didn't push for tetanus shot datails, so he didn't mention the tattoo thing to her. It's becoming clearer to me why this guy is considered a genius.

Carver bends down and whisks dog hair into a dustpan. "Edgar Allan Poe died of rabies."

I try to make shuffling noises with a pile of paper so that I appear busy. "I thought Edgar Allan Poe died of alcoholism."

"I guess he had these weird seizures that made

doctors think he had rabies. He had a bunch of cats, you know." Cats. Figures.

Carver returns the cleaning supplies to the closet and says, "I was going to head down to the beach after work. You want to join me?"

I held his finger for an excessive amount of time today and his jaw just twitched and I'm going to say yes even if I have to spend a lie from the fall account to go. "Yes," I answer. Yes!

Ten minutes before closing time, Carver is back in the kennel run with Vernon. Nina walks into the office. Her blue hair is pinned atop her head like a spiky cactus flower. "Hey, Nattie Girl," she says. She places her elbows on the counter of the reception desk and gives it a knock.

I lean up toward her and whisper, "Do not mention Spud's party. In case my mom walks in."

"Turn your phone on," she says.

I'm hesitant, because doing so would violate the Mom code of cell phone etiquette, but I pull it from my pocket anyway. Nina takes a seat and begins to press buttons.

Her message magically appears on the screen of my phone: MET C AT SPUD'S. HOT! NICE! PERFECT 4 YOU!

I text back. SHHH! HE MIGHT WALK IN.

Nina: MEET ME & K AT RT. 6:30. PIZZA. TALK.

And me: CAN'T. HAVE PLANS WITH C.

Nina reads this and lets out a little whine. OMG! UR

BLUSHING! TTYL. WANT FULL REPORT. I look over at her and smile.

Nina bites her lip, then opens her mouth in a silent scream.

After Nina leaves, Mom emerges from the exam room with her last client of the day, Coco, a scruffy but endearing dwarfish affenpinscher who bounds out, her owner pulling her back as if small Coco has the strength of a Great Dane. I process the payment and print out a receipt of services.

Once Coco's thin claws click on the tile floor out the door, I ask Mom if I can go to Rescued Threads to help Kirby and Eve with inventory.

She looks over her glasses at me. "Be home by nine." I don't push for the extra hour she gave me last night. I know it's early in the summer, but I still have three lies saved up in my annual bank account and have definitely reconsidered spending them according to season. I may just splurge and spend them all this summer!

Carver and I meet at Roberto's, since I want to avoid leaving the clinic together for fear that Mom might notice. We order take-out rolled tacos and two cups of iced ruby red jicama punch.

I feel strangely comfortable with Carver as we walk toward the beach. Normally, when I like a guy, I'm paralyzed by nervousness. But with Carver, even though there's an undercurrent of anxiety, it's not crippling me into silence. I can actually have feelings for Carver and talk to him at the same time: the emotional equivalent of rubbing my tummy while patting my head.

We take our tacos down to the beach, where the torches of evening campfires ignite the fire pits scattered across the sand. The sun still lingers in the sky and beachgoers traipse through the water in their bathing suits.

"I guess we have to steal," says Carver, looking into the distance.

"What do you mean?" I ask.

"Steal campfire. It's no worse than looking at someone's private collection of doll heads," he adds. I laugh.

"Is it illegal?" I'm only half joking.

"Not to my knowledge. Follow me." I match Carver stride for stride as we walk toward the ocean. We reach the perimeter of a family circled around a large fire pit. "Perfect," says Carver, sitting down in the sand. We're about ten feet away from the family.

I kneel down next to Carver. "Are we stealing right now?"

"When the sun goes down, we'll be close enough to the fire for its warmth to reach us. You can't say this isn't the best spot."

He's right. We're nestled on a hill of sand with an unobstructed view of the water. "Yes, it's great," I say softly.

After removing our shoes and socks, we devour our

tacos. Carver struggles a bit because his finger is wrapped in so much gauze. His big toe is still bandaged from the splinter. He's taken a beating the last couple of days.

We talk about Carver's trip to Africa with his mom in the fall and his possibly wanting to delay college for an entire year instead of a semester. "I just feel like I've been on an academic rampage since kindergarten. I want to take a break." He grabs a handful of sand and lets it pour from his cupped hand like an hourglass. "That's one reason I'm here. I wanted to get away from everything I've ever known and go with the flow of something different."

What if he comes back from Africa and decides to live in Beacon? What if he becomes a permanent resident in the room above the garage? What if... "So why do you think Simon bit me?" Carver interrupts my stampeding thoughts. The breeze ruffles his hair.

I wipe my mouth with a napkin. "It depends on who you ask. For instance, my dad would say you'll never be able to answer that question."

"Why is that?"

My toes burrow into the sand. "Well, his theory is that you can never fully tame a dog because the possibility that it will act on instinct is always there."

I stop to look overhead at a swell of pelicans dipping down toward the water. "When Dad lived with us, our dogs had to sleep in these plastic crates at night. It didn't seem right for them to have to be in there, all squashed and caged. Sometimes, in the middle of the night, I'd let them out so they could sleep with me on my bed. In the morning, my dad would be furious. He'd explain to me how important it was that dogs be treated like dogs, not people. He believed that a dog's behavioral problems could be linked back to its owner treating it like a person instead of a dog."

"What do you think?" asks Carver. He's a good listener, makes me feel like he cares about my opinions.

"If you're going to have a dog, it should be part of the family. But I do agree that dogs can never be completely understood by people because we are not dogs. Does that make sense?"

He brushes his hair away from his eyes. "Yeah, it does." Carver is looking at me intently, despite a group of girls in bikinis who are close by. "It's pretty brave of you to disagree with the 'Dog Guru.'"

"Yeah, it's easy to disagree with someone who's hardly ever around." I cough up a slight laugh. "It's funny, because I disagree with my mom about a lot of things, but not about how she handles the dogs."

"I'm just amazed by how the dogs on the exam table allow her to poke and prod them. I've not seen one growl or bare its teeth at her." It's obvious Carver respects her as much as the dogs do.

I turn to watch the water brush along the sand below us. Mom is good with the dogs, probably even more instinctive with and trusting of them than the Dog Guru himself is. If only she could do that with me . . .

I look at Carver, who unleashes an understanding smile, like he's reading my mind. His crooked tooth peeks out from his lips. "Carver? Do you think you could not tell her I was here with you tonight?"

"No problem," he says. Of course he doesn't need to press any further. A week with my mom is more than enough time for anyone to figure out that she's domineering.

Once the sky darkens, the flare of the campfire next to us transforms into a crackling full-fledged blaze. Carver moves a bit nearer to it and motions me toward him. We sit close together, but not close enough to touch. There is so much to learn about him, but sitting here listening to the bumbling waves and fizzing sea spray tells me something, too, in a way words can't. It feels good to be here with him.

The family next to us sit around the fire, their faces lighting up with its glow. We can hear their laughter, their conversation. And as we eavesdrop, I understand what Carver means by "stealing" campfire, because the fire reaches beyond the family surrounding it and spreads to us, where I take it, knowing I'll never be able to give it back.

A leash offers even the worst-behaved dog salvation. —Michael Kaplan, *The Manifesto of Dog*

On Sunday Mom, Grandma, and I attack the dandelions in our yard. (This is one of the only flowers I know by name—and it's a weed.) We are thankful for Carver and his one helping hand; it saves us from being on our knees until midnight.

Never before has weeding been so enjoyable. I think I could be in a swamp of crocodiles and have a good time with Carver. After dinner, we all assemble in the den and join Grandma in watching *The Biography of Lauren Bacall*.

On Monday I walk to the corner to meet Kirby and Nina. Nina leans against the wooden beam of the stop sign. Kirby is not here yet.

"You were supposed to call me!" She pops up from the ground. "Details."

I tell Nina about stealing campfire at the beach. "Did you kiss?" she asks.

"No, but I feel comfortable around him. Like I could eat a bar of chocolate and burp and the earth wouldn't split open."

"Here comes Kirby," Nina says.

Kirby emerges from the fog and walks toward us.

"So you're not returning phone calls?" he asks me when he reaches the stop sign.

"Look," I say, raising my scratched hands. "I spent the entire day yesterday weeding."

"Fine," says Kirby. "But you shouldn't let all this yard work go to your head. You have a responsibility to your friends, after all."

In our cooperative groups at school, we are asked to read Thomas Jefferson's secret message to Congress regarding the Lewis and Clark expedition to explore the West, 1803. Laney gives me dirty looks throughout our reading and sounds angry when she reads aloud the chunk Richard has delegated to her.

Later on, at work, Carver and I swap smiles. We both go back to check on Simon throughout the day, just in case, to make sure he's drinking water and not showing foaming-at-the-mouth signs of a rabid dog.

After work Mom drives Carver and me home, where Grandma has prepared an omelette bar for dinner. The omelettes are perfect, airy and buttery. Carver piles avocado on top of his while I drizzle mine with homemade raspberry sauce.

Instead of going up to his room after our meal, Carver offers to do the dishes. Mom protests, not wanting him to get his bandage wet, but Carver covers it tightly with plastic wrap and persists. This allows me to take Pip, Otto, and Southpaw out for a walk in the fresh summer air.

When I return from walking them down the street, plastic bag of poop and all, Carver is sitting outside on the porch step. He steps into the street to greet me. And on cue, Laney Benning strides out of her house and into the street with us, as if she's some modern-day Lewis and Clark exploring the asphalt and nosing into someone else's territory.

Pip nudges Carver's hand for a rub. Carver obliges. Southpaw commandeers his other hand. Otto uses the full slack of his leash to rush over to Laney and sniff her butt. Laney tries to bat him away, but Otto, staying true to his German shepherd roots, persists in his genetically fearless manner, keeping his nose on the target.

Laney starts to swat at Otto more assertively. "Otto, sit," I say. He walks over to me, panting, and obeys. Southpaw sits next to him quite regally, her long neck graceful, as if she knows full well that her missing leg only adds to her character.

"What's up?" Laney's question is obviously directed at Carver.

"Nothing much," Carver says.

"Want to go for a walk?" she asks.

Carver is stooped down with Pip, who is in dog heaven. Pip's one eye is closed as Carver massages behind his golden ear with his unbit hand. Carver glances at me. "What about you, Natalie? You up for it?" The muscle in his jaw twitches its twitch. Even when he's petting a dog, he is hot.

Laney speaks down at me from atop her dogless high horse. "I doubt you'd want to go where we're going."

Carver looks confused. "Oh. Thought we were just taking a walk."

"We are." She's not telling him the whole truth.

"Come with us," Carver says. I love that he wants me to go. I am so in, too. This is my moment to cross over, to meet Laney where she is. I might have lost some face by backing out of the boob ordeal and buckling under her jabs the past few years, but not this time. I'm playing this game. There's too much to lose if I walk away.

"Okay. I'll just take the dogs in." Laney looks disgusted, like she's just gotten a whiff of bad cheese. Actually, she may have smelled the poop in the plastic bag I'm holding.

I whistle and the dogs file into order.

Once in the house, I dispose of the poop bag, wash my hands, and rush past the den, where Grandma is reading a thick unauthorized biography of the president. Gossip has no boundaries.

"Hi, Grandma." I kiss her cheek as she keeps reading.

The water is running in the bathroom. Mom's in the shower. I dash upstairs, relieved I won't have to look her in the eye. I open the door to the steam-saturated bathroom. "Mom?"

"Yes?"

"Kirby stopped by. Can I go over to Nina's with him to do homework?" Two lies remaining!

The shower curtain slides open and Mom pops out her lathered head, her eyes squeezed shut. "Okay, but be home by nine."

"Thanks."

"And don't forget to bring your phone!" she yells as I close the door.

I grab a sweatshirt from my room, pull my hair from behind my ears, and give myself a once-over in the mirror. I'm hardly Laney Benning. Compared with her, I look like a castaway forced to live without a pair of tweezers or a mascara wand.

I crane my neck to view Laney and Carver across the street through my bedroom window. They're waiting for me on the street, in front of her house.

If I don't go out there, a love affair between Laney and Carver could blossom. In his wedding reception toast, Carver might say something like "At first, I liked Laney as a friend. But a few days later, we fell in love under a streetlight, waiting for some girl—what was her name? Well, she never showed up."

And there I'd be, eyebrows unplucked, at some

table, with Mom and my eleven dogs, who would be whining for bites of my chicken cordon bleu.

Deep breath.

I fling my backpack over my shoulder so that Mom won't find it should she happen to be in my room.

Ready. Set. Go.

Carver, Laney, and I walk in the street: Carver in the middle, Laney and I on either side of him.

"It's so quiet here," says Carver.

"Is that a bad thing?" I ask.

"Why would that be bad?" Laney scrunches her face. It's body language for "You are an idiotic tree shrew for asking such a stupid question." Makes me feel like I'm a kid.

Carver cuts in. "I just meant it's weird." I notice him look at me again. I'm keeping score. "I've always lived around noise. San Francisco is pretty loud. You can always hear an engine roaring or a plane overhead." Then he looks at Laney. I'm sure she's keeping score, too.

We walk another few blocks to Juniper Street and reach a quaint blue clapboard house with a real estate sign sporting a glamour shot of Laney's mom, Trina Benning. A smile that big has to be fake. No one on earth is that happy. Laney stops on a patch of grass. "Shhh," she whispers, "right here."

I know where we are headed. Nina went into the house last week; now it's my turn.

Laney's eyes sweep the neighborhood to be sure all

is clear, and then she leads us to the illuminated porch. Instead of knocking on the door like a normal, polite person might, Laney reaches down to a little lockbox hanging from the doorknob. After she presses a few buttons, the face of the box comes off, revealing a key.

With the key she unlocks the door, and we follow her inside. The hardwood floor creaks beneath us with each progressive step. All of a sudden, I realize that I am off my mother's leash, yet as we get farther into the hollow of the house, I can hear her rattling the collar behind me.

But I keep walking.

19

A dog during play reveals its true nature.

—Michael Kaplan, *The Manifesto of Dog*

The house smells like fresh paint. A single light pours onto a staircase.

Laney escorts us up the steps. A flash of pink underwear sneaks out from under her insanely short skirt. Carver must see it, too.

We enter a room barely lit by the stairwell light.

"Are we trespassing?" I ask. Mom would go into shock if I were caught doing anything that's punishable with fines and probation.

"No, my mom's the real estate agent. I do this all the time," Laney says, like this is normal. "She keeps the access codes on a clipboard in her home office. Besides, I only go in the empty ones." What a saint.

Carver speaks up. "Maybe we should go." Good boy.

Laney walks over to the window, pushes it open,

then strides to the doors of the closet and slides them to one side. "Give me a lift?" she asks Carver. He creates a stirrup with his hands and hoists Laney up so that she can reach behind the top shelf of the closet.

The guy's got integrity, because he doesn't even so much as peek up Laney's skirt.

She dismounts, holding a dark little drawstring bag from which she plucks a tightly rolled cigarette and a lighter.

When dogs feel fear, they bark. Or sniff. Or their hair rises. The hairs on my arms stand at attention. Would getting caught with this involve jail time?

Laney pinches the joint, brings it to her lips, and thumbs the lighter until the hissing flame lights the tip. She closes her eyes and inhales so hard that the smoke must travel to her kneecaps. She holds her breath, then her lips part and a thin wisp of smoke slithers out.

She reaches the joint toward Carver. "Want some?"

He takes it from her and inhales a deep drag, his face caving into contortion. Then he passes it to me.

I hold it between my fingers like some specimen I've just pulled out of a petri dish. My turn.

The stub feels soggy. A head of ash forms, waiting for me to flick it. I don't know how to fake this. Or even if I should fake it.

I pass it right back to Carver. And as if we're playing a nightmare game of hot potato, he won't take it.

"You don't want any?" he asks, baffled.

I shake my head.

Laney tweaks it from me and takes another hit, then holds it out to Carver while her lungs absorb the smoke.

"No, thanks," he says.

She exhales the smoke toward the ceiling. "You can't get high off one toke," she says, sucking in more.

Carver looks at me like he's trying to figure me out.

And I look back, doing the same.

A dog's health reflects its owner's nurturing or lack thereof. —Michael Kaplan, *The Manifesto of Dog*

During the walk home, I try to gain a significant lead on Carver and Laney, but Carver is close behind me, trying to catch up. "Wait!" he yells.

A montage of confusion wraps around me, keeping me from slowing down. I see Mom waggling her finger at me, Dad clicking his clicker to make me heel, Kirby shaking his head in disappointment, Carver asking me to steal more campfire. And I didn't even do anything wrong. Except maybe trespass. And lie to my mother.

What is the matter with me?

We turn onto our street and getting home becomes urgent. I practically do a series of high jumps to get to my front door, and stumble through the wall of dogs who await me there.

Grandma is on her baking stool in the kitchen,

plopping softened pats of butter into a bowl. Her eyes scrunch up when she sees me. "Vhat is vrong?"

I'm about eight feet away from her and somehow she manages to read me. Mom can be an inch away, wearing eyeglasses, and not have a clue.

"Nothing. Nothing's wrong," I say.

"Something is vrong." And with the vigor of an electric mixer, Grandma twirls her wooden spoon, transforming flour, sugar, and egg into creamy cake batter. Normally, I'd eagerly swipe a finger along the rim of the bowl. But not tonight.

The dogs totter upstairs with me to Mom's room, where she is splayed on her bed, holding an issue of *National Geographic*. I keep a safe distance from her, worried that I reek of secondhand smoke. "I'm home."

Mom looks at the clock on her nightstand. "It's only eight-thirty. You had till nine." She must be surprised, because when she gives me an inch, I usually take it. Mom puts her magazine on her lap.

Oh, no, please don't let her pat the mattress for me to come and sit down next to her. "You left your keys in the door earlier. I shouldn't have to remind you that you need to be more responsible. For God's sake, you're sixteen." She sighs in frustration. "I put them on your dresser."

I had to screw up something. My mouth comes to the rescue with a yawn.

"Love you," she says as I leave the room. She clicks off her bedside lamp.

"Me too." I doubt she hears me, because after lights-out, she is the kind of person who fades into dead sleep when her head hits the pillow.

The dogs go into my room, but I stop outside Mom's door and press my back against the wall.

I'm her—the girl in the made-for-television drama. The one who dodges the doobie, the one all the adults of the world applaud because she "just said no." Oprah will call me to be on her show featuring Teens Who Don't (a panel of probably five people my age). My peers in the audience and watching from home will flip me the finger.

Southpaw pokes her head out my bedroom door, curious about why I'm not in there yet. She dodders over to me. I slide down the wall, get on all fours, and crawl into my room with her, petting Fu-Fu for good measure. I climb onto my bed, tug the covers over me, and create a cave.

Scores of people my age are probably congregating near a bong or popping little pink pills into their bodies right now. This whole pot thing should be no big deal. One could do something a lot worse, like leave her keys dangling in the front doorknob.

Southpaw jumps onto my bed. I tuck her under the covers with me and scratch the coarse hair on her back. Her thumping leg tells me she's grateful.

I reach into my backpack, fumbling for the phone. Nina answers on the first ring.

"I have to talk to you."

"Shoot, sugar. You okay?"

"I went for a walk with Carver and Laney. She took us to that house. You know, the one you went into last week."

"Yep. So what happened?"

"They smoked pot."

"Did you freak?" Nina asks after a thoughtful pause.

"Kind of."

"Do you remember that I've had my share of it?"

"Yeah, but you said it made you paranoid."

"It did, but not everyone gets the same kind of high. So did you say something to them?"

"No, but I ran away from them when we were walking home."

"Why?"

"I don't know. I was uncomfortable. I guess seeing Carver do it sort of surprised me."

"So you really like this guy?" Nina says with a coy lilt in her voice.

"I do. I admit it. But what if he's some pothead?"

"Then maybe you'll end up not liking him. He probably does it once in a while, like me. You don't think I'm a pothead, do you?"

"No," I answer.

"You want to know what I think?"

"I called you, didn't I?"

"You're careful about stuff, and that's fine. And I totally love that you are still friends with me even though I'm not as careful as you. But I do think you, Natalie, are scared shitless."

I feel stung. "Scared of what?"

"Look, I know you think for yourself. I've heard enough arguments between you and Kirby to know that. But ever since I've known you, you've been making up little lies to avoid the wrath of your mom."

"If I didn't, I'd have no social life," I say defensively.

Nina is kind enough to ignore the pinched tone of my voice. "Right, and that's fine, too. But, and please don't get pissed off at me for saying this, okay? You wanted my opinion."

"Say it."

"You don't stand up to her. Not like you should go ape shit or anything, but if you don't start speaking up for yourself, you're going to lie yourself into someone you're not. You can't see everything through your mom's eyes."

"So what should I do, ask my mom for permission to trespass and date a guy who dabbles in pot?"

"No, I'm not saying that. I just think that sometimes you confuse what your mom thinks with what you think. What does your gut tell you about Carver?"

I think for a minute. "There's this thing I've never felt before. I spent last week making up great excuses

137

not to like him. But he's nice, different. I feel a connection with him or something."

"Is that your final answer?" Nina asks.

"Yes," I say.

"Sleep on that, okay?"

"Thanks, Nina."

"I loves you."

"Loves you, too." I smile and flip my phone closed.

I took Mom into that house with me tonight and ran home with my tail between my legs. Nina's right. I'm not sure where Mom's opinions end and mine begin.

But I might be ready to find out.

Dogs competing for pack dominance must be separated. —Michael Kaplan, *The Manifesto of Dog*

Tuesday morning, after Mr. Klinefelter gives us a lecture about the Louisiana Purchase Treaty of 1803, he asks us to spend forty-five minutes in our cooperative groups looking closely at the treaty and assessing how the acquisition of 828,000 square miles of land, purchased at less than four cents an acre, added to Thomas Jefferson's "Empire of Liberty."

Allison yawns when Richard asks her to contribute her opinion. Laney looks directly at me and says, "It sounds like Thomas Jefferson manipulated Napoleon for the land." Laney is defending Napoleon. It is also a direct stab at me, I assume, because she glares at me even after she says it. Yeah, me and big bad Thomas Jefferson. Sheesh.

Walking to work after school is becoming its own

minidrama. I travel from the roots of America's history to the modern-day scene of life in a dog clinic, both nervous and thrilled about seeing Carver.

Vernon is behind the reception desk when I get there. "Hey, little lady. What's going on?"

"Nothing much. School." I go behind the desk and drop my backpack onto the floor. "I swear my history book weighs as much as a Saint Bernard."

"Does it drool, too?" Vernon asks.

I laugh. "Luckily, no."

"Your mom's in the back room spaying Tinkerbell. Carver's back there, too," he says.

I take the needed precautions: I scrub my hands, then grab a face mask and loop the straps over my ears. Mom and Carver, also masked, hover over Tinkerbell in the surgery room. She's a fluffy white Maltese who is anesthetized, sprawled on her back, and gently strapped to a little dog gurney. Mom's gloved hands are about to make an incision into Tinkerbell's shaved belly but stop when she sees me.

"I'm here," I say behind my mask.

Carver and I exchange stifled hellos.

"How was school?" Mom's hands are still positioned for surgery.

"Fine. Just wanted to let you know I was here."

"Grandma needs a ride to the Elks' lodge tonight. You'll need to pick her up by six o'clock."

"Sure." She seems to be in a good mood. "Can I go

to Quimby's while I wait?" I'm trying to flex some courage and exercise my right to musical enrichment.

"No, I'm not comfortable with you driving around by yourself." Thanks to network television's *Everyday Dangers* for that segment on the hazards of teens driving alone at night.

I push it a little more. "But it's only a few blocks away."

Carver cuts in from behind his mask. "I've been wanting to go there. I hear they have an amazing collection of vinyl." I wonder who told him that.

Mom relaxes her arms for a minute to think. Tinkerbell's bubble-gum pink tongue peeks out from her slightly tapered muzzle.

Please, Mom, I mouth underneath my mask. *Please.*

"Okay, Carver. Why don't you go along with Natalie?" Yip! If my mom knew what Carver was doing last night, she'd probably wrap him up in postal tape and send him back to San Francisco.

"As long as it's okay with Natalie," Carver says.

"It's fine," I say.

I try to act like Tinkerbell, sort of laid-back and going with the flow, as one would be if she were sedated and about to have her girl parts removed. I don't want Mom to catch on to the fact that she's just granted me my ultimate wish for the day. Now that I think about it, I realize that she probably would have let me go to the beach with him the other night, too, because he's

Boy Wonder in her eyes. She had her "boundaries" talk with me, and because Carver looks so good on paper, he's sort of duped her.

I should have figured that an SAT-top-one-percenter could do no wrong in Mom's eyes.

"We'll need to leave here at five-fifty," I say, bull-horning that I, too, am capable of being responsible.

Mom starts the incision on Tinkerbell's bare stomach. I detect a grin behind Carver's mask before he is pulled into the intrigue of dog surgery. I walk away carrying the souvenir of Carver's hidden smile.

At five-thirty, Nigel St. Paul, a healthy Chow Chow with a mane of auburn hair, and his elderly owner, Mrs. St. Paul, are waiting in the reception area for Mom to finish with a patient. Nigel is panting and slobbering a pool of drool onto the floor. His black tongue extends and retracts like a scroll of rubber that won't stay rolled. His curled tail wobbles side to side when the front door opens. All of us turn our heads.

Laney and Maryann walk into the office with their short skirts and matching wrist purses. Twins. They reel back when they see the waterfall pouring from Nigel's mouth.

"I don't have Bogart," I say curtly.

"I know." Maryann is chewing a huge wad of gum. "Your friend had him. Again. We got him back today." Kirby's mom must have made him return Bogart.

Laney places her little purse on the counter of the

reception desk. Because her shirt isn't long enough, her belly button peeks out like a little cyclops eye. "Is Carver here?"

"Just a minute," I reply in a professional tone. I'm interested in knowing what she wants with Carver. I get up and go into the back to find him. He's mopping up a dog kennel.

I stay back at the mouth of the kennel run. "Carver?"

"Yeah?" He stops mopping and wipes his forehead with the back of his bandaged-finger hand.

"Laney's here to see you." I say this as if she's a client, but I know she'd never have enough character to own a dog, or, for that matter, a cat.

"Hey, can we talk about last night?" he asks. My shoulders relax. Laney's waiting for him, and he wants to talk to me.

"Yeah," I say, but I can hear Mom calling.

"Natalie?" She comes in behind me. "The phone was ringing. You missed the call."

"Sorry. I was getting Carver." I walk toward the front with Mom and Carver trailing behind.

Laney and Maryann greet Carver with an open spigot of sap-drenched charm. Nigel, Mrs. St. Paul, and Mom remain in the reception area with us. Maryann introduces herself to Mom while I cringe and feign interest in filing folders alphabetically behind the reception desk.

"What are you doing tonight?" Laney asks Carver

through a smile that's supposed to look casual but is clearly fake.

"I'm going to Quimby's with Natalie." *Score!* I think. I realize I'm being petty, but he's doing something with me. Na, na, na, na, na!

"You girls are welcome to go along," Mom says. Perhaps she has inhaled too much ether.

Wait, that's not it. Mom thinks Maryann is an honor student and a responsible treasurer for the Good Samaritan Society (because of the pre–slumber party lie I told). Mom thinks these girls are a good influence, despite their go-go-dancing-length clothing.

Laney faces my mom. "Thank you, Mrs. Kaplan. That's so thoughtful." Phony.

Mom turns her attention to Maryann now. "And thank you, Maryann, for inviting Natalie to your slumber party." What? Am I like six or something? I am now shoving files into the filing cabinet, not even paying attention to alphabetization. This is so unfair. She won't let me drive even Kirby and Nina around in the car.

"Natalie?" Mom asks.

"Me?" I ask back. For a minute, I thought she was pretending I wasn't even standing here, so that she could monopolize my social life.

"Drive safely." Mom gently leads Nigel and Mrs. St. Paul into the exam room and gives me a this-is-so-great-that-I'm-a-cool-enough-mom-to-let-you-drive-with-your-friends-in-the-car look.

144

I give her a could-you-be-more-blind-to-the-fact-that-I'd-rather-drive-in-the-car-with-a-load-of-dirty-jockstrap-wearing-red-assed-monkeys-than-with-Laney-and-Maryann-in-the-backseat? look.

Now Carver, Laney, and Maryann occupy the reception area. They are waiting for me to happily accompany them to the car.

The legendary German shepherd Rin Tin Tin was able to survive a World War I bombing and then go on to star in twenty-six films; I can certainly try to forge my way through this outing. "I need a few minutes," I tell them. "I'll meet you outside by the car."

In the bathroom, I splash my face with cool water from the tap and look in the mirror. My cheeks could use some blush, my invisible eyelashes could use some mascara, and my pale lips could use some lipstick. At least there's a flash of blue coming from my hair. And this is no time for self-deprecation.

Laney's just a person wearing a bitchy mask. Or a bitch wearing a human mask, no offense to the female canines of the world. Either way, I can't let her get to me.

There's also the issue of Carver. He's either going to prove himself to be a jerk or not. It's worth finding out, because my brain and my body are in an intense wrestling match: my hormones really don't care that much about the pot smoking; they just want me to get some action. My brain, or the part of my brain that wants my room back, is repelled by the idea that he might be a pothead and is still leery of him.

When I get outside, Carver, Laney, and Maryann are standing around the car. I climb in first and unlock the back doors, watching through the rearview mirror as they load into the backseat, Laney getting in first, Maryann following. Carver goes around to the passenger seat to sit next to me in the front, earning a point for the bodily team. Go h'mones!

Carver and Maryann fasten their seat belts. Laney doesn't and looks straight ahead. I glance at her in the rearview. "Laney, I could get a ticket if you don't wear your seat belt." With a dramatic sigh, Laney fastens up.

We drive out of the lot and onto 101. I'll bet Mom has a vision of me tootling around with a carload of honor society members, the future Ivy Leaguers of America. She probably thinks we are engrossed in some Mensa-inspired trivia as we drive. I can hear her now: "Natalie, don't answer the question about the theory of relativity while you're driving! Wait until you are at a complete stop." She is so deluded!

Maryann sniffs. "It stinks in here." Little does she know that she and Laney are sitting on the hair-infested area typically reserved for Pip, Otto, and Southpaw. Vindication at last.

"I wasn't even sure you had a driver's license," says Laney. She knows I drive.

"I like to walk," I say, leaving out the part about Mom not letting me use the car if I'm not doing her some favor.

We turn toward the train tracks. "Where are we going? Quimby's is back there," Laney says.

"Oh, yeah. I forgot to tell you." I peer at her again in the rearview mirror. "We have to pick up my grandma first." I may not have the strength to scare a flea off a hairy flank, but my grandma can instill fear in anyone. Even these two in the backseat.

A pup prematurely separated from its mother is doomed. —Michael Kaplan, *The Manifesto of Dog*

Grandma is waiting at the curb when we get to my house. I'm not running too late tonight, but I'm pretty sure the extra passengers in the car will annoy her.

Carver steps out to help Grandma into the car. "I do not need help!" She waves him away, but he stays there until she's safely inside.

Grandma turns her body to glare into the backseat. "Vhy are they here?" Looking at them in the rearview mirror again, I can see that Laney and Maryann are caught off guard, scared even. Just a minute ago, they were poised, posture perfect. Now they are slumped down a bit; their skin hangs more loosely from their tight faces.

Staying true to character, Grandma highlights each upcoming turn toward our destination with a glass-shattering "Here!" and a firm pointing of her finger.

"Stop!" she shouts when I veer the car into the Elks' lodge parking lot. Grandma turns to the backseat and says, "Don't be late."

Carver ignores Grandma's insistence that she walk to the entrance alone and follows her through the door of the Elk's lodge. Chivalry is not dead! The hormones are in the lead! It's now 2 and 0.

When we pull into the small overloaded parking lot of Quimby's, Maryann makes an observation which I didn't think her capable of. "Looks like you have to park on the street."

Since the car is at a standstill, Laney opens the door. "Why don't you drop us off?" She and Maryann get out. "C'mon, Carver."

"I'll go with Natalie." He is saving me from humiliation. And although I am no stranger to being humiliated, it sure feels good to have someone on my side. A big pom-pom twirl for the team who scored another point! Yeah, hormones! Win! Win! Win!

Laney shuts the door and stands frozen with Maryann as I step on the gas and drive out of the parking lot. Thoughts of stranding them here come to mind, but instead, I search for a parking place on the street.

"Sorry about last night," Carver says.

I spot a space along the curb and pull into it. "Why?"

"Because you probably felt uncomfortable," he answers.

Am I that easy to read? "What makes you say that?" I turn off the engine.

"You ran home, number one. And you didn't smoke any."

"Do you have a problem with that?"

"No, but I thought you'd have a problem with me doing it, since you didn't."

"I do wonder why you took a puff and then stopped." My thumbs wrestle each other on the steering wheel.

We both look straight ahead and watch a group of black-clad kids from my high school jaywalk across the street and over to Quimby's. Carver then turns to me. "So you want to know why I didn't have more?"

I turn to him now and our eyes meet. He says, "I didn't want to disappoint you." That totally sounded like something I would say. Maybe we are more alike than I realize.

"Why do you care if you disappoint me?" I ask.

"Because I like you." He likes me. The sweat above my upper lip reappears like someone Etch A Sketched it there. "I've smoked weed before. It takes me outside of myself."

I have no idea what he means. "Why would you want to be outside of yourself?"

"It's something that frees me, lets my mind relax." Isn't that what yoga is for? "I sort of get that feeling

150

with you. The feeling that I can be myself without having to think too hard about it."

"But I've been rude to you. And we haven't spent that much time together."

"You forgave me for feeding your dog chocolate. You took care of my finger." He raises it for me to see. "You stole campfire with me." He leans in closer to me, the warmth of his breath fogging up any common sense left in my brain. "I'm comfortable with you."

We'll be connected if I so much as pucker. And because the hormones are in the lead and I'm relaxed and Pixie has just twisted herself into lotus position for a session of meditation, my eyes close and it happens. Lips touch, a little moist and very soft. The tip of his tongue roves over to mine. We tilt our heads for a better fit. His hand brushes against my cheek and eases down to cradle my chin.

If anyone ever asks me what it's like to fall in love, I will describe this moment, right now, when I can feel a part of myself letting go, falling, to meet this other person halfway.

There's a tap on the window. Carver and I pull slowly away from each other.

Laney and Maryann are motioning us to get out of the car. I let out a big and breathy sigh. Lust is very real when you are up close and feeling it.

I lean over and whisper into Carver's ear. "We'd better get out of the car."

He whispers back, his lips touching the lobe of my ear. "Okay, but just so you know, I'd rather stay here."

When we step out onto the sidewalk, Laney stands still, like a statue. She's probably shocked to see that I've kissed someone and maybe even more shocked that the someone I was kissing is someone she likes. Carver makes an effort to walk next to me.

I look at my watch before we go into Quimby's. "I'm going to the used-album aisle. Let's meet back at the car at seven-thirty." I never knew one kiss could arouse so much confidence!

I spend the entire Quimby's time with Carver, flipping through the comfort of albums. I don't pay attention to the Queen album or the Janis Joplin album. No, I am wrapped up in this guy who is standing next to me. I don't even mind that Laney and Maryann keep hovering, popping their heads into the aisle to spy on us. They couldn't be more obvious if they were holding binoculars and wearing camouflage.

Carver's flawed, but he's honest. And I pulsate when I'm next to him.

Maryann and Laney are already waiting for us when Carver and I get to the car. I reach into my backpack for my keys.

"We're here on time," Laney snaps, as if I inconvenienced them by making them wait. I shake my bag a few times and listen for the jingle that always helps me find my keys. No jingle.

"Maybe you left them in the car," says Maryann. She stands on tiptoes with Laney and they look through the passenger window.

Laney releases a hideous witch cackle. "I guess you were too distracted to take them out."

I peer into the car and see the keys dangling from the ignition. I look at my watch. Five minutes to get Grandma.

"Aggh!" I yell. "I can't believe this!"

"I can." Laney crosses her arms over her cantaloupes.

"No big deal," says Carver. "Just call your mom. She has an extra set, right?"

He doesn't completely understand my mom just yet.

"No matter what, I've got to run over to the lodge so my grandma won't be wondering where we are." She is going to go ballistic.

"I'm fast; I'll do it. We'll just wait till you get there. In the meantime, you call your mom and get the keys," Carver says. Without a response from me, he starts running down the sidewalk toward the lodge a few blocks down.

Laney looks at me like I am a pathetic lawn gnome. "C'mon, Maryann. We'll find a way home." They swivel around and swing toward Quimby's.

I reach inside my bag for my cell. It's likely that I deserve all this. I mean, I lied to Mom, trespassed. I've even allowed myself to have feelings for Carver. The universe must be punishing me. Either that or Fu-Fu is not getting her share of rubbing.

I press the silver square buttons on the phone to call Mom at home and prepare for the you're-so-irresponsible-I-can't-trust-you-if-you-can't-even-keep-track-of-keys-you're-never-driving-the-car-again lecture from Mom. She'll remind me that Grandpa used to carry a spare set of keys in his pocket. Grandpa's walk always chimed with the jangle of spare keys.

Thankful for the image of him with his bulked-up trouser pockets, I turn off the phone before Mom has a chance to answer. Maybe remembering is not the solution to forgetfulness, or, as Mom would call it, irresponsibility. Maybe a good backup plan is the key.

23

A dog can't achieve biochemical balance without daily exercise.

—Michael Kaplan, *The Manifesto of Dog*

I hardly qualify as Balto running on all fours through the freezing temperatures of Alaska, delivering medicine to diphtheria victims, but the six-minute five-block run to the clinic leaves me panting and feeling victorious.

Vernon unlocks the door, wearing his latex flea-treatment gloves.

"Hey, Nat. What're you doing here?"

"I forgot something."

"C'mon in, then." He lifts his hands in the air. "When I was your age, I never imagined a normal night would involve giving a bearded collie a flea dip."

"It's a noble pursuit, Vernon," I say. "The dogs of the world are lucky to have you."

"Thanks," he says with a chuckle.

"I'll just be a second." In Mom's office I open the top drawer for the spare keys. Cornered inside the desk drawer is a picture of me when I was about eight years old. I'm smiling a grin of big pre-orthodontic awkward teeth and holding Troy in my lap while he licks my chin.

The picture makes me want to cry. No matter how much I try to escape her, I still feel trapped inside that little girl.

I grab the keys out of the drawer and run back into the reception area.

"You get what you need?" Vernon asks. If he only knew.

"Yep. Have a good night."

I'm officially eight minutes late now. Never before have I been so grateful that I wear running shoes. They are the superhero cape of my wardrobe.

I sprint back to the car, kick it into gear, and zoom to the lodge.

A cluster of elderly people stand outside, sipping from Styrofoam cups. Carver is among them, talking. Grandma is listening along with the others. She doesn't even notice the rumbling of the car as I edge up to the curb.

Carver notices me, though. Grandma allows him to take her cup and her purse and they both walk toward the Land Cruiser. I've never seen Grandma surrender anything, especially her purse. One would think it was a bag of diamonds the way she holds on to it.

I'm even more shocked when he opens the door for her and she doesn't protest.

"You are late," she says to me.

This may be the very first time in my life that I've heard my grandma utter an understatement.

When we get home, I check in with Mom, who turns her light off when I leave the room.

I'm down to my last lie. (Getting the spare keys from the clinic equals one.) Tonight is going to be two for two, because I allow myself to accept the invitation from Carver to go up to the room, his room.

Carrying the turntable, the speakers, and some albums, I quietly make a few trips from my room to the steps outside. Carver meets me at the bottom of the stairs each trip and transports the goods upstairs.

After we set up the turntable and speakers, Carver and I lie on the hard wooden floor, looking up at the shimmering specks on the ceiling created by the disco ball. My thoughts about Laney and pot smoking are on the ceiling, dots I can no longer connect because all I care about right now is being here with Carver. Our shoulders graze and swap messages in body heat.

Listening to a record is much different than hearing a CD or a tape. The needle never leaves the vinyl, so the pause between songs is filled with anticipation.

"This is such a great song. Jethro Tull's best," Carver says. Lead singer Ian Anderson, backed by lively acoustic guitar and flute, sings:

> *One day you'll wake up in the present day—*
> *A million generations removed from expectations*
> *Of being who you really want to be.*

I could request a soundtrack that's slow, something that would evoke romance and passion, but this is oddly perfect. The music fits the nimble specks of light being projected by the disco ball.

"These are the albums you'd want if you were stranded on a desert island," Carver says through a sigh.

"Yeah, I guess I'm the island my dad deserted," I say. "What about your dad?"

"My dad is still having an affair with a boat. He's a journalist for a travel magazine. But that just gives him an excuse to sail. I don't see him much, either. At least your dad left you some music."

Our thumbs rub together. The slow motion of Carver leaning toward me suggests the beginning of a kiss. I close my eyes, allowing his lips to surprise mine. We are connected, nose to nose, chin to chin. I try to memorize the moment, trace the tingle of my fingertips down to my ankles. My bones disappear. There is only tenderness.

One kiss and our heads roll slowly away from each other, our eyes back to the ceiling, but our hands keep holding on.

24

Grooming a dog for vanity's sake violates its personal space.

—Michael Kaplan, *The Manifesto of Dog*

Brett Holifax's coming at me like a fish darting for food does not count as a kiss. It happened during freshman year and it was a one-way kiss that was unlike any fantasy I'd had of what a kiss should be. It was slobbery, reckless, and unwanted.

Now that I've had a real kiss, I make a mental note of what qualifies as a good kiss: A good kiss is soft. A good kiss has a soundtrack, a song or a sound that can trigger the memory of the kiss. A good kiss is mutual. A good kiss is pure, performed exclusively as a kiss, without the pressure of being felt up, or down. A good kiss defines itself immediately and requires no debate about whether or not it is or isn't a good kiss; it simply is, without a doubt, a good kiss.

Wednesday morning I cram myself through my assigned homework while eating some cereal, then head to the corner, where Nina is waiting. Nina is beyond punctual. She beats the second hand to its mark on the clock.

"What gives?" asks Nina when I approach the stop sign smiling.

I sit down on the concrete, not holding back this time but telling her everything, because telling her everything is like thinking about it.

Before class, I veer from Nina and Kirby toward the bathroom. Laney and Maryann enter as I'm washing my hands. They both stand in front of the mirrors and begin their makeup ritual.

Laney dabs her lips with a spongy pink-tipped applicator. "So," she says, "Kyle picked us up last night, since you couldn't drive us home, but I couldn't help noticing your car was miraculously gone when we came out of Quimby's."

"Yeah," I say, tugging a paper towel from its dispenser. "I had a spare set of keys at the clinic."

Laney smacks her lips. "That's convenient."

I need to push through my fear of this girl. "Not really. I had to run and get them," I say.

Laney says, "Well, we figured it was your way of getting Carver all to yourself."

"I wasn't trying to get him to myself."

Laney tilts her head to the right. "Whatever." Yeah,

whatever. Like I need a *plan* to be forgetful. She and Maryann pivot out of the bathroom. I give them enough of a lead that it looks like I'm not following.

After school I walk toward work, thinking about how Carver's and my taste buds touched last night. My hands tremble as I get closer to the clinic. Before last night, I had never shared a good kiss with anyone, let alone faced the aftermath of it. Will we pretend it didn't happen? Or will we fling directly into a saucy kiss when our eyes meet?

When I get there, Carver is out to lunch. I am both relieved and disappointed. While Mom is in the exam room, I am able to slip her spare keys into her office.

A half hour later, Lollipop, a bloodhound whose head seems too burdensome to lift from the ground, waits in the reception area. His name obviously came from the small boy sitting next to him on the floor.

Carver returns from lunch holding a brown paper bag. He steps over Lollipop on his way to the desk. Why he makes my skin quiver, I don't know, but he does and it's quivering now.

"Hey," I say when he leans over the reception counter and places the paper bag in front of me. I wonder what's in there, but the kid next to Lollipop is picking his nose with his pinkie and staring at us. It's sort of distracting.

"Go ahead and look," Carver says. I peek inside the bag and find a huge cookie. "It's peanut butter chocolate chip. One of the best I've ever had."

"Don't tell my grandma that." I smile widely, reach in, and break off a piece. It melts in my mouth. "Yum."

"Keep it."

"Really?" He's giving me his cookie and I'm acting like it's an engagement ring. "Thanks."

"Wanna hang out tonight?"

It's time to introduce him to Nina and Kirby. "My friends and I are getting together for soup. It's our Wednesday-night thing. Why don't you come along?"

"Soup." He slowly nods. "Sounds good." Carver is making this easy for me. He doesn't even ask why we're eating soup in the summertime.

"We're meeting around seven, so we can just go from my house."

Carver suddenly turns to catch the nose-picking kid in his stare. It's so sudden that Lollipop manages to raise his head off the ground. His dewlap dangles from his double chin, in the middle of his chest. The boy's finger stays lodged in his nose, stuck to whatever is inside.

Night rolls around like molasses globbing off a spoon. At the clinic I plod through my homework to free myself from having to do it early in the morning.

Mom drives Carver and me home. This time

Carver sits in front with my mom. She explains euthanasia to him while I steal glimpses of the left side of his face, paying particular attention to the way the soft hairs on his neck make a swirling design.

After taking the dogs for a walk, I spend the better part of an hour attempting to apply mascara and eyeliner. Feeling like a clown, I remove it and settle on maroon-tinted Chap Stick. The skin around my eyes is blotchy and red from wiping off the eye stuff. I slide into my favorite jeans. From downstairs, the smell of something baking wafts up to my room.

Expecting to find Grandma, I'm surprised when I see Mom at the kitchen table paying bills. I stand beside her. "Tonight's soup night," I say.

"Just give me a few minutes, and I'll give you a ride."

I'm out of lies and am going to try something else. "Carver's going with us. Can I walk there with him?"

"And you're meeting Nina and Kirby there?"

"Yep."

"Is he coming by here first?" I nod. "Call me if you need a ride home." She stuffs a check into an envelope. "Walk safely," she says, "and be home by nine."

MOM LETTING ME WALK WITH CARVER TO MIGUEL'S : SHOCKING : : MOM NOT LETTING ME WALK WITH CARVER : EXPECTED. "Thanks,"

I say. This is unprecedented trust in me. Was it my report card or did Mom undergo a lobotomy?

"Natalie?" Mom says as I start to walk out of the kitchen. I turn to look at her, waiting for a "just kidding!" "Remember what we talked about? Boundaries."

"I remember." End of conversation. But there it is! I still get to go. She is beginning to trust me. La, la, la!

A few minutes later, a knock on the door triggers a last-minute dash to the living room mirror. The red marks on my face have faded, so at least I don't look like I got into a brawl with a cat.

I round the corner to the entry hall but stop short before Mom and Carver see me. Mom has gotten to the door first. She is muttering something to Carver but she's loud enough that I can hear the refrain, the babble that I've had to hear my entire life. Words like "expectations" and "cautious." Phrases in the key of "let's keep it professional" and "you are a guest in our home."

So much for trusting me.

After she's finished, she calls for me and I go to her like a dutiful subject.

"Ready?" Carver asks. He looks good: jeans, light blue T-shirt with white long-sleeved jersey underneath, messy hair.

I look at Mom, who is standing between Carver and me, apparently proud that she has marked her territory. The dogs stand behind her, because she is the alpha of our pack.

"I'm ready," I tell Carver. Then I walk past Mom, leaving her absorbed in her world and stepping outside to assume control of my own.

Edible rewards imprison the full potential of a dog. —Michael Kaplan, *The Manifesto of Dog*

I seriously consider grabbing Carver's hand and pulling him up to the room above the garage, where we can swap kisses on the floor and I can search for his tattoo, but I'm able to restrain myself (unfortunately).

Carver holds my hand in his. We stroll on the sidewalk. The sky begins to turn purple; the stars twinkle behind the haze. There's a nice chill in the air, the kind that makes you feel glad to have someone to hold on to. "Your hands are so soft," says Carver.

"That's a miracle considering how many times I wash them at work." Dog slobber and hair are occupational hazards. "You know, I should tell you that my friend Kirby is sort of opinionated, but don't let him scare you." The guy deserves fair warning.

At the stop sign, Carver grabs hold of my other

hand, bringing me near him. We face each other and he leans in for a kiss. Slow, soft. He smells like he belongs here, in nighttime and sea-salted air. I can't believe that last week I was trying to think him out of my head.

Carver slowly pulls his lips away. "Don't worry about me," he says.

Frequent stops for kissing fuel us toward Miguel's.

At the restaurant, we walk through a corridor of bright blue walls into a dimly lit dining room. Tissue-papered donkey-shaped piñatas hang from the ceiling, and candlelight dances inside globes of red glass centered on each table.

Kirby and Nina are waiting at a booth, sitting across from each other. Nina waves us over like she's hailing a cab in a crowded city. "Bonjour!" she says. Kirby scowls in his seat.

"Hi, Carver," Nina says enthusiastically. He says hi back. I love this girl. She can make anyone feel at home in her presence.

"Carver, this is Kirby," I say. Kirby acknowledges Carver with a testosterone-loaded nod.

"Here, you two sit together." Nina moves over to Kirby's side of the table. Carver motions me to go first into our side of the booth, where we settle in, thighs touching. "Kirby and I already ordered a Mexican pizza for us to share, without onions," she says to me, "since you dislike them."

"Thank you very much." We scan the menu.

La sopa especial of the night is Spicy Tortilla. Carver and I order the special. Kirby rolls his eyes and orders meatball soup, out of spite, I'm sure.

After we order, Nina scoops her chip in salsa and says, as eloquently as one can with a mouthful of food, "Carver, you've got to tell us what it's like living in San Francisco. Do you ever visit Haight-Ashbury? My dad is a total Dead Head, which is sort of weird because he's a military man, but he probably saw the Grateful Dead a hundred times in concert before Jerry Garcia died." She says this so rapidly that it's amazing the food stays inside her mouth.

Kirby says, "It's customary to breathe when you talk, Nina." She sticks her tortilla chip–laden tongue out at him.

Carver says, "We live about a fifteen-minute walk from there." He puts his hand on my knee. It feels so natural, so comforting.

"I don't get it," Kirby says, not touching the chips and salsa he usually devours. "Why 'the Grateful Dead'? Grateful to be dead?" Oh man, he's gonna be argumentative.

Carver seems immune to Kirby's cockiness. "Actually, Jerry Garcia opened up the dictionary one day and there it was, grateful dead. It's based on a story about a guy who gives his last penny to help some stranger get buried. The penny-giver becomes a hero and the buried dead, grateful."

I feel proud that Carver is not only kind but also

knowledgeable about his music. "I never knew that," I say. "Just think, Nina, all this time your dad lectured us about the Grateful Dead and he never explained this one. We'll have to brag to him that we know something he may not."

"Enlightening." Kirby sighs. "I'm going to go see where our pizza is. Scoot, Nina." Nina gets out of the way for Kirby to exit the booth. He disappears into the waiter's area and our server comes out carrying a huge tray with our pizza.

"I'll go get Kirby," I say, wishing I could take Carver's hand with me. Carver moves so that I can get out of the booth.

I find Kirby in the small entryway to the kitchen, where he stands looking at his feet. Nina was the one who wanted to meet Carver, not Kirby. The clanging of pots and the sizzling of food waft from the kitchen. "Kirb?" He looks at me. "What's your problem?"

"I don't trust him."

"What? You don't even know him." I lean against the wall, next to Kirby, letting a hurried server through. "Can't you for once let someone make an impression on you before you go impressing your opinion on them?" I feel like I'm pleading. I tone it down a bit. "Don't you trust me, Kirby? His being here is a result of my forming my own opinion, which, by the way, I thought you valued."

He looks into the kitchen and watches a cook chop tomatoes on a butcher block at fast-forward speed. I don't understand Kirby right now. "He just doesn't seem like your type."

"And this is based on saying hello to him? You haven't even attempted conversation yet."

"I can just tell, Natalie."

"And what is my type?"

"Smart. Funny."

"I'll have you know that Carver is both. He's fun to talk to. And he's easygoing. He makes me feel good about myself. So stop acting like a turd." I look at our table to peek at Carver and notice that our food is being served.

I tap Kirby on the shoulder. "Our pizza is at the table," I say, walking back to our booth. Kirby straggles behind.

"Very effective, Kirby," Nina says. "As soon as you left, the pizza arrived." Kirby sits and grabs a slice. I'm thankful his mouth will be busy for the next few minutes with something besides negative commentary.

As we chew our pizza, a loud voice echoes through the door of the restaurant. Then she appears.

"Ha! Look, Maryann, it's Carrrrver! And Nina!" Laney shouts, running over to our table as if she's leaning toward the finish line of a race. Her little pink purse sways helplessly from her wrist.

Not that everything was running smoothly in the first place, but Laney's being here raises the chances of things getting worse.

Laney slaps her hands down on the table. "I

loooove this pizza." She smells like a liquor cabinet. Maryann lurks directly behind her like a shadow.

"You okay, Laney?" Carver asks.

"You are soooooo sweet!" she says back breathily.

Kirby wipes off his arm with a napkin. "Do you mind? You're sort of spraying spit all over my pizza."

Laney looks down at him, confused. "You're always mad or something. Lighten up." Wrong. Thing. To. Say.

"Uh, no," says Kirby. "It's just that I never order saliva as a topping." Laney laughs and actually conjures up a bona fide snort.

"You're kind of cute. I've never noticed that before," she tells Kirby matter-of-factly. Then, without permission, she reaches for Kirby's slice of pizza and dips it into her mouth.

"Sure, go ahead and help yourself," Kirby says sarcastically.

Nina swings in. "Laney, you're drunk. Quiet down a bit." Nina really does care about Laney, which makes me feel sort of bad about not caring. "We can walk it off outside or something." She lowers her voice to a whisper. "Everyone is staring at you."

Laney turns around, confirming that this is true. She shrugs and takes another bite of pizza.

Nina leans into us. "Let's get her outside so she doesn't have such a captive audience."

Carver goes to fetch our check and pays for "our" part of the bill. *Our* part!

By the time we make it outside, Laney has gone from obnoxious to lethargic. We congregate around a bench. Laney places a hand over her stomach. "I don't feel so good." Kirby and Carver direct Laney to sit on the bench. Kirby remains seated with her while Carver unhinges himself and sidles over to Nina and me.

"What are we going to do?" I ask. "How long does it take someone to sober up?"

"I've never seen her so drunk," Nina says. Laney's head rests on Kirby's shoulder.

"Well," says Carver, "we've got to get her somewhere safe, where she can snap out of it. It'd probably be easiest if we took her to my place." My place? He cares about Laney after all. This is something a close friend would say, not an acquaintance.

Or am I being selfish? You can't leave someone drunk sitting on a bench and expect that they'll make it home. Right?

"Oh, yeah. Natalie's mom would love that," Kirby says with a snicker.

"We could party over at Laney's house. No one's home," says Maryann, obviously out of it. Kirby lets out another snide laugh.

Nina stands next to Maryann and says in a soothing voice, "Maryann. We are not going to 'party.' We're trying to figure out what to do with Laney here because she's partied too much already."

"Oh," Maryann says, unfazed.

"We can't leave her alone," says Carver.

"It's fine. My mom won't have to know," I say with a wobbly tone of conviction. "We'll just have to be quiet about it. I'll go in the house and talk to her while you guys get Laney upstairs."

I can justify this. It's no different from saving a dog in distress. No different than giving it water, nursing it back to stability. From my track record, this is one thing I know I do quite well.

Chewing is passive-aggressive dogspeak for "I need attention."

—Michael Kaplan, *The Manifesto of Dog*

The burden of getting Laney to walk the mile to my house is a heavy one. Kirby and Carver stand on either side of her, helping her to balance just in case she should stumble, which seems likely, since she has gone from a stroll to a saunter.

As we trail them, Nina mouths, *Are you okay?* I give a slight nod. Then she raises her eyebrows and twitches her head toward Carver. *He is so hot!* she mouths. Yep.

We make it to my place after eight-thirty p.m. To sustain our covert operation, I try to assume a business-as-usual cool by walking into my house while the rest of the group steers Laney into Carver's room.

"I'm home," I say, entering the den, where Mom

and Grandma are watching vintage black-and-white footage of Julia Child smashing the soft insides of potatoes with a utensil that looks like a small pitchfork. I sit on the floor in front of the television, trying to pet all the dogs at once to distract them from any hullabaloo by the garage.

On the screen, Julia Child grips a skillet with both hands and says in a deep, masculine voice, "When you flip anything, you must have the courage of your convictions."

"You're early again." Mom's perky, because she thinks I'm going the extra mile in her little obedience game. "Is Carver home, too?" she asks. I nod.

"Shhh!" says Grandma, who is listening to the gospel of Julia Child. I watch for a few more minutes.

"I'm going to take the dogs out," I whisper.

"Don't go far," Mom says. "Stay on our street." Easy enough.

The dogs and I make it up to the room, where Laney is propped like a life-size rag doll on the futon, her eyes closed. Nina hovers over her with a washcloth. Maryann sits on the floor, staring at Laney. Southpaw hops over to Maryann, who cringes. Carver's in the bathroom with the door open, wetting another cloth in the sink. The dogs sniff each corner and settle on the floor with Kirby for some affection.

"How is she?" I ask Nina.

"Ugh," says Laney.

Nina shrugs. "That just about sums it up."

176

Carver gives Nina a fresh washcloth. Laney curls her body into a tight ball. "I want to go home."

"Nope," says Carver, "got to sober up first."

"Turn on the disco ball, will ya?" Nina asks. "That, by the way"—Nina points to the disco ball—"was my idea, remember?" The first time Nina saw this room, she did utter "disco ball."

Carver turns off the main light, flicks on the blue spotlight, and gets the ball spinning. Snowy specks splatter the ceiling in a circular pattern. Laney looks up, her head circling while tracking the disco ball. "I'm gonna be sick." Carver swoops her up in his arms while Nina and I run ahead to the bathroom.

Laney kneels in front of the toilet. "Get out, Carver," she says. He shuts the door behind him, leaving Nina and me with Laney.

Nina rubs Laney's back. "Let it come out." With a loud squawk, Laney heaves into the toilet. "Good," says Nina, like a true coach. I grab another washcloth from under the sink, wet it, and hand it to Nina. Laney takes it and wipes her mouth.

"I have to take the dogs back in the house," I say, aware that my time is limited. "I'll come back when it's safe."

"Hey, grab some crackers, will you?" asks Nina. "She'll need something in her stomach." Laney hovers over the toilet again, her body writhing as she throws up.

A video of someone puking curds of cheese into a

white porcelain toilet might be the ultimate antidrug campaign.

I herd the dogs back into the house. The credits of the Julia Child show flip on the screen while Mom and Grandma get up from their places on the couch. "I'm going to bed," says Mom.

"Me too." Grandma shuffles over to me, holds my head in her hands, and kisses me on the cheek. "Pumpkin cake is in the kitchen. Tomorrow I make something with potatoes!"

I settle myself on the couch and grab the remote. "I'm gonna watch some TV."

"Night." Mom leans over and kisses the top of my head. I watch the beginning monologue of an old *Saturday Night Live* rerun, waiting a solid eight minutes before snatching some crackers from the kitchen. I also steal a few bites of Grandma's moist cake before sneaking outside with the dogs.

"They're still in there," says Carver when he opens the door for me. The disco ball keeps on spinning.

"She sounds like a wounded bear," Kirby adds. Maryann still sits on the floor. Her head wearily dangles atop her neck as she fights sleep.

I tap on the bathroom door. "Nina?" The door opens and Nina looks pale. Laney is crouched, her head resting between her arms, which are propped on the rim of the toilet. The smell emanating from the bathroom is sour.

"I need a little break," says Nina. "Think I'm gonna toss some cookies myself."

I hand Nina the package of crackers. "I'll stay with her."

"Laney," says Nina, "I'll be back in a few minutes. Natalie's here."

"Uh-huh," Laney manages to moan.

It seems awkward to rub Laney's back like Nina did, so I just stand behind her. She lets out a long whine, lifts herself, and throws up again. Long threads of spit sway from her lips. She reaches over to flush, but the handle comes loose.

"I'll get it." Stretching over Laney, I lift the lid of the toilet tank and set it on the sink. A yank of the chain and the toilet flushes. But there, among the mechanics of toilet fixture and rising water, is a plastic Ziploc bag duct-taped to the inside of the tank. It's filled with what look like grass clippings. At this point, I know better.

This can belong only to Carver. I rip the bag from its place, give it a quick drying-off with a hand towel, and shove it into my jeans' pocket. Laney is slumped down on the floor, unable to see me.

I replace the lid and twist the handle of the flusher back into its place, securing it tightly. I flush again, and the tornado of water in the toilet funnels down, getting slurped into the hole.

Laney makes her way out of the bathroom and

collapses onto the futon. Seeing me in the open doorway of the bathroom, Pip and Otto shuffle to attention.

"Lucy in the Sky with Diamonds" plays softly on the turntable, and everything in the room except for the orbiting droplets of light from the disco ball comes to a photographic standstill. Maryann is in a childlike trance. Nina feeds crackers to Laney as if she's offering Communion. Kirby hides behind the *Sgt. Pepper's Lonely Hearts Club Band* album cover. And Carver sits near the door leading outside, petting Southpaw. All 110 pounds of her sprawls across his lap.

I am no Lucy in the sky with diamonds. There are no marmalade skies or marshmallow pies, only a disco ball and saltines. Carver looks up at me. I am holding his secret in my pocket, asking him with my plain, nonkaleidoscopic brown eyes to bare himself, show me who he is so that I can trust him.

The song ends, and as if he himself is here to offer a segue, Paul McCartney starts singing "Getting Better," the next track on the record.

"I want my bed," Laney says, snapping the room back to reality.

Carver lifts the heavy weight of Southpaw off his lap. She does a one-pawed downward dog stretch and walks over to Pip and Otto. "I think it's okay now," Carver says. He says to Laney, "I'll walk you and Maryann over to your house."

"Nina, I'll walk you home," says Kirby. Nina and Kirby get to stay out until eleven-thirty. "I don't want to miss my ten o'clock *Twilight Zone* rerun. Not that this zone of ours hasn't been interesting."

"I'd better go in." I motion the dogs over to me.

"Bye, Nattie," Nina says. Kirby gives me a stiff wave, like he's saluting me.

"I'll walk you out," says Carver. We stand on the landing outside the door. The dogs are eager to walk down the steps and into the house.

"See you tomorrow?" he says.

"Yeah." He leans in for a kiss. I turn my head and give him my cheek.

"Are you mad about this?" he asks. "It would have been wrong to leave her alone." Thank you, Mr. Nightingale.

"Of course," I say. "I'm just beat."

"Good night, then."

"Night." I can feel him watching me as I head down the stairs.

Back in the house, I turn off the TV and go up to my room. Mom's light is on, her door cracked. I shut my bedroom door behind me, pry the clear bag out of my pocket, and sit on my bed, crunching the bag between my hands.

It's two a.m. I'm still awake. The little bag of horror is hidden inside the cavity of Fu-Fu. Right now, attempts to sleep are futile. I keep hearing Julia Child and that

181

thing about flipping with the courage of your convictions.

Just when I think Carver's this great guy, some zinger comes flying into the picture, making me question whether he is who I think he is. Does he deal? Did he brave the airport with the pot in his luggage? And if he did, how did he get past the drug-sniffing German shepherds? Will my dogs smell the bag and lead Mom up here in a drug bust?

I'm dizzy from the constant whirl of questions.

This is what I know: Carver makes me feel different than anyone else I've ever been around has.

I wedge my arm under Fu-Fu's scratchy underside and grab the baggy. Not bothering to strap on a bra or change out of my tank top and pajama bottoms, I leave the dogs in their lump on my bed and tiptoe in the darkness down the stairs, out of the house, and back to Carver's room.

The lights are out; he's sleeping.

I look up to see the white saucer of the moon. Suddenly, I'm scared. Am I jumping at this too fast, like the Russians did when they sent Laika, part Siberian husky, to orbit earth in the 1950s? They had it all planned, how they'd rocket the dog into space, but there was no plan for getting her back to earth.

What is my plan here? What will I do once I hand over this little bag? Stomp out of the room? Cry? Tap dance?

Laika died of fright after the rocket launched her

into space. I'm scared, too, but putting it into perspective, I'm not scared enough to die of fear.

Conviction!

I tap gently on the door until I'm forced to knock more loudly. Carver opens the door in sweatpants and bare chest. The wedge of light from the moon illuminates his tight belly and muscles. There is no marijuana leaf tattooed across his chest (thank goodness). He looks warm and wrinkled from sleep. Conviction, Natalie, not muscle, I think.

"Hey," he says, scratching his head; his hair is confused in different directions.

I walk into the dark room, plastic bag in hand. Carver shuts the door and sits on the edge of the futon, on top of a ruffled comforter. I stand in front of him and toss him the baggy.

He catches it. "Whoa," he says groggily. "How did you get this?"

"Why were you hiding it?"

"But, wait." He shakes his head. "Why did you take it?"

"If it's not important to you, why do you care?"

Our questions chase each other around the room until we are tired. Carver buries his head in his hands. "Laney gave it to me. I haven't even touched it yet."

"Yet?" I ask.

"Yeah, yet." He rubs his eyes. "I was planning on having a little here and there. It's summer. I graduated. I just wanted to kick back."

Of course I understand this part of it, because I, too, often have visions of taking a vacation from myself.

The blue part of my hair dangles in my eye. I wrap it behind my ear. "I don't think it's the pot that bothers me. But it's deceptive, you know? You roll into town under the banner of Boy Wonder and then here you are hiding pot in the toilet." I keep going, because I am not scared anymore. "And the other night, when we were in the car, you told me you didn't have any more because you didn't want to disappoint me. Did you mean that?"

"I haven't done it since." He reaches his hands out to me. I take a step back. "I like you, Natalie. It's not that important to me. It looks like a bigger deal than it actually is."

"I'm trying to figure you out. You say it's not important and then you have like a year's supply of it hidden in the toilet."

He stands up with the bag in one hand and motions me to follow him with his other hand. "Come here."

He walks me toward the bathroom. I've spent more time in this bathroom than I'd prefer tonight. He lifts the toilet seat and dumps the contents of the baggy without spilling on the rim of the bowl. With a flush, the water swirls with what looks like oregano and disappears. "See, I don't need it."

"I wasn't asking you to do that," I say. "I just want

to be able to trust that you're who I think you are, that's all."

Taking my hand in his, he leads me to the futon, where we face each other. "This is who I am." He rests his hands on my waist, his body slopes toward mine, warmth collects between us, and we kiss, folding onto the comfortable cushion of the futon mattress.

Our bodies shift so that we are side by side, our heads sharing the pillow. Carver holds me, his mouth still connected to mine; our tongues touch in soft, spiraling rhythm. Time turns into a series of movements.

Carver's mouth leaves mine, but his lips don't leave my skin. They trace my cheek and travel down toward the nape of my neck. My fingertips explore his shoulder blades and slide down the smooth skin that travels the measure of his back. Carver's hands reciprocate. One tousles my hair; the other reaches cautiously under my shirt. It caresses the span of my stomach and veers to the side, up toward my rib cage, creating a pulse inside me that is moving more than blood.

His hand crawls farther up and up, and right before he gets to where I think he's going, I place my hand on his. Our hands tighten together. We kiss like this until his hand descends the slope of my torso to my hips, where his arms encircle me.

I've never been in anyone's arms this long. Long enough to fall asleep.

Dogs, like rebel children, need defined boundaries. —Michael Kaplan, *The Manifesto of Dog*

A series of knocks on the door, quick and hard, then slow and pounding, wakes me. My eyes open. Darkness has been replaced by light. I'm still in Carver's bed. With Carver!

I look at his wristwatch: 6:30. Thursday morning.

It could have been a nice moment, waking up together. Maybe we'd kiss each other, though I'd be sure to hold back my morning breath.

But the knocking is beyond disruptive. And worse, I know who is behind the door. Carver places his hand on my arm. "We didn't do anything wrong," he says, eyes shut. His body turns away as if he is going back to sleep.

I sit up. "I'm in your bed." Fully clothed, my shirt hiked up only a bit, but still.

He sits up now, rubbing the sleep from his eyes. The knocking becomes desperate.

I should hide in the closet right now, cash in my remaining lies, and scuffle out when Mom leaves. But I get up to answer the door, because I don't know the secret passageway out of that kind of lie.

I open the door and face her. Mom stands in her gray sweats. Her hands are in fists and bolted to her hips. Her frizzy hair makes her look like a madwoman who is clearly ready to eat her young. "What. Are. You. Doing. Up. Here?" She can barely breathe.

"I fell asleep, Mom. We were talking, and I fell asleep."

"No," she says irately. "Last I saw, you were on the couch, watching television, and then I assumed that you went to sleep. In your room. In your bed."

Carver comes up behind me, wearing sweatpants but no shirt. The bare-chested look worked well last night but seems a bit sketchy now with Mom at the door. "Sorry, Elizabeth, but it's true. We just fell asleep."

Mom cranes her neck past me, toward Carver. "No, Carver. I trusted you. Both of you."

"I left something here and came back to get it," I explain.

"Don't lie to me!" Her nostrils are flaring. "Let's go." She pinches the back of my neck and practically forces me down the staircase.

A second after we go inside the house, Mom whips

me around to face her and points a stiff finger in my face. "Even though you may feel that sixteen is old enough to make your own decisions, you need to know that you are my daughter, living in my home, where there are boundaries. Boundaries that you have violated, young lady." Mom shakes her hands in rage.

"Nothing happened! It's not like we had sex."

"You, Natalie, were in a boy's bed—"

"Yes, but—"

"But what? When Faith and I agreed that Carver could come and stay here, I didn't think that I'd have to worry about the two of you. Especially you."

"If that's true, then why did you come up to the room in the first place? Why did you give me the 'boundaries' speeches?"

"You were up there, Natalie. You're proving my point. I can't trust you." What have I been the last sixteen years if not honest? I understand that I lie, but my lies are weak, tweaks and twists of truth so that Mom won't have to worry about me. And this is what I get in return.

I push back. "Then why would you allow a guy my age, a good-looking one, to come and live with us? It's a no-brainer, Mom."

"Don't use that tone with me, Natalie." She turns away from me. "Go up to your room, because I can't look at you right now."

Mom put the dogs outside, so I have no allies, but there is the smell of cinnamon drifting in from the kitchen, a sign that Grandma is there. I want to bury myself in the coffee cake she's probably pulling out of the oven right now. Instead, I follow Mom's instructions and walk up the stairway, holding on to the railing for support.

Mom has the nerve to make me feel shameful about this. And shame is the worst. She could slap me across the face, and it wouldn't hurt as bad as this feeling of shame.

I enter my room and dive onto my bed, stubbing my toe on Fu-Fu once again. My pillow takes a punch, and I plunge my face into it, giving it a scream. I pound my fists on the mattress.

Sooner than I can string my thoughts together, Mom bursts into my room. She begins to pace back and forth in the tiny space between my nightstand and my closet—three steps forward, turn, three steps back. "You are not ready for this," she says.

At this point I'm sitting straight up on my bed with my pillow balled in my lap. "Ready for what, Mom? I told you, I didn't have sex with him."

Three steps forward, turn, three steps back. "Maybe not, but it's all part of a chain of events. They all lead to something, to expectations. You can't be dense about this." Mom stops midstep, looks out my window at the room above the garage, then shoots her eyes back at me. "You are wrong if you think I'm going to stand here and allow you to ruin your life by going too far with this boy!"

"Don't you trust me?" I ask.

She walks toward me. "No!" There it is, the golden goose egg of truth tottering between us. "I was once your age. Emotions rule over logic."

I lean up into her face. "Nothing happened, Mom. Don't you think I know about consequence? Haven't you crammed these little talks into my head long enough for me to know that?" Tears start to spill. I shrink back and hover over my pillow, shaking my head. I hate that I cry when I'm angry. "You don't give me any credit."

She ignores me and keeps going with her own distorted view of this. "You have violated my trust." She steps closer to me. I look up at her; the fire in her eyes is close enough to burn mine. "That, Natalie, is the bottom line."

We are locked on each other right now, our heads squared on the same plane. I tilt my head, wipe the tears from my eyes with my wrists, and try to shift the imbalance of the situation. "Is this about Dad cheating on you? Is that why you can't trust me?"

Mom's mouth loosens. She reels back a bit in disbelief, and then her mouth wrenches into tightness again. "This has nothing to do with your father, Natalie!" I don't believe her. "I don't want you and Carver alone together." She cuts the air with her flat hand. "You are grounded." Here it comes: for life. "You'll come straight home after work every day."

Tears come back in full force. "For how long?"

"Don't ask." Mom turns toward the door.

"I can see why Dad cheated on you!" I shout. Mom stands frozen, her hand on the doorknob, her back facing me, and I keep going because I know it will hurt. "You forced him into a corner, just like you're forcing me. The only way out is to lie. Or to leave."

Mom doesn't turn around, doesn't even lash back. Enough time passes that I could apologize to her for what I've just said. But I won't. When she realizes this, she walks out of the room, quietly shutting the door behind her.

28

**The pitch of the bark, not the bark itself, conveys
the message.** —Michael Kaplan, *The Manifesto of Dog*

That morning I wait until the last possible moment to
leave my room, anticipating a firing squad on the
other side of my door.

I finally make my way down the staircase. I don't
even go around to the back to check on the dogs. I
just beeline toward the door, skipping breakfast and a
kiss from Grandma out of sheer and utter fear of my
own mother.

I'm just thankful right now to the foggy heavens
above for summer school.

I hurry past my driveway but slow down enough to
look longingly at the room above the garage. The
shades are drawn. I'm already worried about facing
my mom again, but should she ask Carver to leave, it
will be more impossible.

Winning the title of First One to the Stop Sign, I slump against the splintering wood and wait.

"What's wrong?" Nina asks when she arrives a few minutes later. "Did your mom find out about Laney?"

"No, much worse."

She joins me on the concrete. "Tell." And I do.

"Whoa, Nattie," she says after I give her a summary. "First of all, very brave of you—your going up there and confronting Carver about the weed."

"Yeah, but look where it got me. My mom is freaking out, and I'm going to be grounded so long, I'll probably sprout roots."

"But there's something to be said for your going to him for the truth."

When Kirby arrives, Nina gives him a shortened version. In the spirit of my mother, he says, "I told you I didn't trust him."

"Ugh!" I walk a quick pace ahead of Nina and Kirby. They jog behind, trying to keep up.

Kirby pleads. "Sorry! Just trying to make you feel better." I turn to face him. He almost falls backward. "I'll stop. Immediately."

"Thank you." I slow down so that we're walking together on the sidewalk.

"Wow, though," Kirby says. "You on restriction? It's sort of like Snow White being charged with possession of crack."

"I guess I'm not as angelic as you think."

Kirby starts up again. "Hmm. What are you hiding there, Natalie? Is there something else I should know about you and Carver? Tell us what really happened between you two last night."

Feeling like a provoked pit bull terrier, I lash back at Kirby. "Why are you being such a jackass? You just told me you were going to stop with all of this!"

Nina gently slides between us. "Settle down, you two. Kirb, give the girl a break, huh?" He throws up his hands in defeat. Smart move, considering the lengths a pit bull will go to to protect herself.

Laney and Maryann are not in class when we arrive. Three seats in a row are free. Nina points and says, "Tic, tac, toe."

Mr. Klinefelter walks into the room and steps up to his podium. "Good morning. Today we are going to double back a bit on our time line. Hence, I ask you, what could be more beautiful than the Bill of Rights?" Mr. Klinefelter leads into his lecture on the Bill of Rights. Toward the end, he asks if we have any questions. Kirby raises his hand. "I'm listening to all these rights, Mr. Klinefelter, and what I don't understand is why people our age, under eighteen, don't get to enjoy a lot of them."

Bingo! I'm expected to act like an adult, be responsible, but any idea I have that doesn't meet Mom's approval warrants lecture and, now, restriction. I'm living under a different set of rights. The truth: until we are eighteen, we live under the constitution drafted by our parents.

"Elaborate, Kirby, please," says Mr. Klinefelter.

"Take freedom of speech. We can't go around saying what we want. I've seen more than one person thrown out of a classroom for cursing, yet we're told we have freedom of speech? We don't."

"There!" says Mr. Klinefelter, stabbing the air with his flicked-up thumb. "An excellent point, young man. Even with the freedom of speech in place, people used to get arrested for using profanity within earshot of women and children."

"Yeah, but that doesn't make sense," says Kirby. "Don't we have the right to say what we want?"

"We're looking at two different issues here. First, because those under eighteen aren't of 'legal' age, there are loopholes. Second, it's important to remember that your rights end where another person's begin. You may have the right to say something profane, but I have the right not to hear it. And there's the rub."

Rub, indeed.

"Test tomorrow on the first five chapters!" We groan, because, well, we can't curse about it.

My phone starts barking no more than a minute after we're released from class. "You'd better walk directly to work right now." Mom.

I follow her instructions, walking to work with fingers crossed in hopes that Carver is still employed.

When I get to the clinic that afternoon, Hamlet, a young and hyper Dalmatian, waits in the reception area with his owner, Mr. Stoop.

Some names just don't seem to fit. Dogs are victims of their owners' propensities. Mr. Stoop probably decided a long time ago that he would someday get a dog and call him Hamlet. (No matter that Shakespeare's Hamlet was a depressed stoic.) This black-spotted blur of energy, who is pouncing up to slurp my face, is no Hamlet.

I check in with Mom, as she has dictated I do. After today's class, I've resolved that I live under a dictatorship. Once Mom and Vernon are in the exam room with Hamlet, I rush to the back, hoping to find Carver.

I can't see him when I enter the corridor of the kennel run, but I am relieved to hear him. His tone is low and sweet. He says, "That's a good boy." When I find him in the kennel with Simon, I consider that my mom probably locked him in there as punishment. I wouldn't put it past her. But to my amazement, Simon, who earlier in the week thrashed at Carver with a nip, has his head in Carver's lap.

"How in the world have you tamed this dog?" I ask, standing behind the chain-link gate.

"The last couple of days, he's allowed me to get closer. Of course, this helps." Carver pulls some jerky bits from his pocket and allows Simon to eat out of his cupped hand. Dad would shudder and click his training clicker at Carver. According to the Dog Guru, a dog should behave for you, not for food.

"Well, I'm impressed. You're not feeding him chocolate."

"I'm glad you're here." He walks out of Simon's kennel and over to me. Simon whines at the edge of his gate. "It's okay, boy."

Carver faces me and holds my hands in his. He kisses me, a small delicious peck but a bold move, considering that this is Mom's territory and we're not supposed to be alone together.

"I apologized to your mom again. She said to keep it professional and what's done is done. That I need to focus on work, not you." He clears his throat. "She asked me to call my mom and tell her about last night."

"Sounds like her. I'm surprised you're still here." I tighten my grip on his hands to let him know I'm happy about his being here. Mom is giving him a second chance, which makes me feel bad for thumping her so hard with the comment about Dad. Not bad enough to apologize, though.

"Well, I got an earful from my mom."

"What did she say?" I ask.

"That I am a guest. I need to respect your space." Carver touches his nose to the tip of my nose.

"Is your mom going to make you come home?" Pixie becomes an anchor on my heart.

"No, my mom knows we didn't do anything. She just told me to be more sensitive to your mom's limits."

I pull back from him, but our hands stay locked together. "So what part of my mother's brain is missing? If your mom is cool about it, why can't mine be?"

"My mom has always been a friend, I guess. Your mom is more of a—" He hesitates.

"What? Control freak? Warden?"

"No, she's just more protective of you."

"Speaking of which, I'd better get back up to the front." If she sees us talking, alone, I may be forced to wear a chastity belt.

"Come here for a second," Carver says. He brings me in closer. Perhaps the smell of Science Diet Adult Chicken and Rice Recipe emanating from stainless steel pet bowls, the gray cinder block walls, and the slobbering sound of dog aren't the most romantic sensory details, but it doesn't matter. This is romantic. This feels right and good. We kiss, letting our tongues play a quick game of footsies. "We'll figure something out," he says. And I believe him.

Products such as dog strollers are entrapments, not necessities.

—Michael Kaplan, *The Manifesto of Dog*

Restriction has one thing going for it: test prep. There's plenty of time to study when you are caged inside the house.

Friday, test day, has something going for it, too: there is no cooperative group.

The rest of the weekend is marked by the monotony of staring at my bedroom walls. The dogs have never been so important to me. I've even noticed them being distant from Mom, like they are taking sides.

One thing is clear, though. Restriction is counterproductive. It does not make a person reconsider her actions. I am not feeling guilt like I have the past couple of weeks when I was knitting my white lies. No, with each passing moment of restriction, I am concocting blueprints of escape routes and offenses that will free me. I may as well wad them up and toss them in the garbage, because I lack the intestinal fortitude (aka guts) to execute my plans.

And another thing: distance really makes the heart grow fonder. I miss Carver. At work we have devised a circuit of communication by leaving notes for each other in the kibble bin.

Sunday is the worst, because there is no work or school to keep me busy. By Sunday night, Carver has given up waiting for me. Around eight p.m., he leaves his room and scuttles down the steps and into the world without me. He gets home by ten-thirty that night, and I go to bed wondering where he went.

Walking to school on Monday, I vicariously live through Nina and Kirby as they recount a Saturday-night jaunt to La Paloma Theatre for a viewing of *The Rocky Horror Picture Show*.

"I saw Carver last night," says Nina, avoiding a crack in the sidewalk.

"Where?" I ask.

"Peter Pole played a gig at Quimby's. He went with us."

Kirby doesn't say a word. "Us?" I say. "As in you and Laney?"

"And Maryann," Nina adds. "I know what you're thinking, Natalie. You have nothing to worry about.

Carver played it cool and mentioned at one point he wished you were there."

"No way," mutters Kirby.

I look at him. "'No way' what?"

"Guys don't say that," he responds.

Nina and I stop. Kirby walks ahead a few steps and then spins around when he notices he's alone.

"So you think I'm lying?" Nina says, prickling up. He'd better watch it. There're two of us and one of him.

"No, it's just that he's trying to prove something. Like he has to say that, so you'll report back to Natalie with reassuring news."

I place my hands on my hips. "What's wrong with that?"

"It doesn't seem genuine. If you had a good relationship, you'd trust him," says Kirby.

"I didn't say I don't trust him," I snap.

"Kirby, do not put matters of the heart on your resume. You clearly don't get this stuff," says Nina. "Let's keep walking."

During cooperative group we are supposed to be compiling pros and cons of state versus federal regulation of commerce, an offshoot of Mr. Klinefelter's lecture on *Gibbons v. Ogden*, 1824. Richard asks me to take notes for our position on pros and asks Laney to record the cons. "I saw Carver last night," she says.

My nerves start to rumble. She is bullying me. "Good," I reply.

"Let's just start with what we know." Richard

ignores Laney's side conversation. "With the invention of the steamboat in 1807—"

Laney interrupts. "Why weren't you there?"

"I'm on restriction."

"Can you two discuss this some other time?" asks Richard.

"Let 'em talk," says Allison, looking from me to Laney. Richard shakes his head but quickly joins Allison as a spectator of the conversation between Laney and me.

"Why are you on restriction?" Laney asks.

How dare she! She should be nice to me. Does she not remember that she puked in my toilet?

And it's on the tip of my tongue: that I'm on restriction because Carver and I were found in bed together, that we're crazy about each other, that we will run away together to San Francisco, where he will reveal his tattoo. We will run a halfway house for abused dogs and live happily ever after.

But I don't say anything. Instead, I crown myself with a tiara of cowardice.

After class, Carver is waiting on a concrete bench in the quad area. The sun overhead glazes his honey blond hair. He sits cross-legged, the hems of his faded jeans frayed, his smile made even more perfect by that tilted eyetooth of his.

Pixie, who seems to be wearing ice skates today, does a triple toe loop jump. I run over to Carver. "What are you doing here?"

He takes my hands, gives them a squeeze, and pulls me so close that I am forced to arch my back to avoid tumbling on top of him. "I'm taking my lunch break. I wanted to know if you'd like to join me for a field trip tomorrow."

"How? I have school and then work." I touch the tip of his nose. "Oh yeah, I'm grounded, too, remember?" My phone starts barking. Mom is insane! I pull back from him. "My mom is calling. Just a sec," I say to Carver.

"I'm on my way," I grunt into the phone.

"Good," Mom grunts back.

I hang up and get back to Carver. "Walk with me?"

"That was my plan. I'll veer off to grab some lunch before we get there."

I wave good-bye to Nina and Kirby, who are watching me from the vending machines.

Carver entwines his fingers with mine. We cross through the parking lot, toward the sidewalk. "You were saying something about a field trip?"

"Would you be willing to miss school tomorrow?" Carver asks.

"Yes," I say, even though I'm not sure how I'm going to forge an excuse note.

"Good." He squeezes my hand again. "I have tomorrow morning off."

"How did you manage that?"

"I asked your mom."

"That's original." Now I get it: ask the woman

directly instead of using the trapdoor of seasonal lies! Except I've tried that before. I'm surprised that Mom hasn't tightened her stranglehold on Carver, especially since he's riding on the fumes of a second chance.

"I told her I wanted to go to the botanical gardens."

"So where are we actually going?" The ice skates Pixie is wearing start to cut a nervous hole into my stomach.

"To the botanical gardens." He looks at me as if this should be obvious. "I want you to come with me." This makes it easier to say yes. I am not ditching school so that we can rent a hotel room and have hot, steamy sex. No, I am skipping class so that I can commune with nature (and Carver) at the botanical gardens. Don't degrees of wrongdoing matter in this world?

Our plan goes from seed to bloom. Tomorrow morning, Tuesday, I will walk toward school. Carver will intercept me at Clove Street, and we will then walk the one-point-something miles to the botanical gardens. They open at eight-thirty a.m., and we'll stay till eleven-thirty a.m. Afterward, we'll both walk toward work but fork off from each other before we get there so as not to raise any suspicion.

At work I snag a few pieces of Mom's letterhead for the absence note I will give to the attendance office when I return to school on Wednesday. For once I'm thankful that I can hardly decipher Mom's handwriting, because as far as forging a note goes, this shouldn't be too hard.

I'm so excited I can hardly breathe.

Hardly breathing may not be an ideal breathing pattern.

Monday night I'm hammered with an epidemic of second thoughts. What if Mom finds out? What if Mr. Klinefelter kicks me out of class for ditching? My excitement has turned to fear, but I try to relax my breathing and keep my eye on the first-place prize of this outing: Carver.

When I walk toward the corner on Tuesday morning, my worry resurfaces like the dry patch on Pip's back. No matter how much salve we rub on him or how many omega-3 tablets he ingests, the red and irritated bald spot keeps returning. But I push myself forward, ignoring thoughts of reform school or military school for daughters who lie to their mothers.

I meet Nina and Kirby at the corner and am about to tell them I won't be joining them when the huge bug-covered grille of my mom's car halts at our stop sign. Mom must be going back home for something. She opens the window. "I'll give you kids a ride. Jump in."

No!

This is classic Mom. For once in my life, I would like her not to be generous when the moment warrants such generosity. Carver is waiting on Clove Street! What am I going to do? The three of us pile into the backseat of the car. Immediately, I roll down the window, perching my chin on it for air.

Mom chauffeurs us to school, answering Nina's question about the ear woes of her cat Mitzi. Mom assumes it's ear mites, and although I don't want to seem insensitive, I want out of the car so that I can sprint to the corner of Clove and Carver!

Mom drops us off. Kirby and Nina thank her and spill out of the car. I climb out last. Mom is waiting for me to say thank you, but I'm too upset and defeated to deliver.

"See you after school," Mom says before I shut the door.

I nod and watch her drive until I see the last glimpse of the white car leaving the parking lot. I'm afraid that if I start running toward Clove, Mom will catch me like I'm a mouse trapped in a maze experiment. There's no telling what streets she'll take on her way home and then back to work.

"Natalie? Are you coming?" Nina asks. She and Kirby wait at the entrance of the school.

Without an answer, I follow them onto the school grounds, away from Clove Street, and into the classroom. Pixie must be dead, because there is nothing in my stomach but the weight of a lead bowling ball.

Projecting human traits onto dogs results in dysfunctional behavior.

—Michael Kaplan, *The Manifesto of Dog*

Forty-five minutes into class, as our cooperative groups slide desks into clusters, I tell Mr. Klinefelter that I'm not feeling well. He excuses me from class, so I head out the front entrance of the school. Then I tightly secure my backpack to my shoulders and start running.

I dash to the corner of Clove and Carver, where there is no Carver. Catching my breath, I quickly text Kirby, telling him that I'm okay and that I'll talk to him and Nina tomorrow. This averts any possibility of them calling the clinic or my house to see where I've gone.

From Clove Street, I run until I approach the entry kiosk of the botanical gardens. After I pay my five-dollar admission fee, I walk up the driveway toward the entrance, wiping the sweat from my forehead with my sweatshirt before tying it to my waist.

For years I have lived in Beacon and have never been here. Dogs are my world, not plants. But when I walk onto the premises I'm captivated by the octopus's garden of plant life. Thin trees, thick trees, small trees, tall trees, bright blooms, pastels, shrubs, bushes, and vines. It looks like something out of a Dr. Seuss book. I can't believe that all of this green and growth is hidden from the passersby on the street.

I walk down a concrete path into another diverse patch of trees, hoping to spot Carver sitting Christopher Robin–style underneath one of them. There are trees I've never seen before. One tree in particular at the bottom of the path catches my attention. It's huge, towering about thirty feet in the air. The bark looks like cork. I step off the path so that I can touch it. Its stump is light and feels hollow, like Styrofoam. It's hard to believe that such a huge tree can feel so fragile.

Back on the path, I keep walking until I am struggling up an incline. On each side of me are the blossoming heads of flowers. I've never had such a strong urge to know the names of plants. I want to point and say, "Ooh, look at those lovely peonies," and, "The coloring of those rhododendron is spectacular," but I don't know what to think other than "Those are pretty pink flowers, and I like those droopy purple ones hanging along the vine."

I decide then and there that I am going to commit the names of flowers to memory.

My search for Carver continues as I follow the rise of the path. I hear a faint spray of water, and as I walk forward, it seems to transform into a downpour. I round a corner, then stop on a deck perched at the side of a waterfall. Ribbons of water tumble over rocks, creating a narrow flood below that continues beyond view.

Then I realize: where there is water, there are fish. I quickly skitter down a set of stairs shouldering the trail of water to the bottom, where it has settled from its journey into a still pool.

At the edge of the pool is a boy—the boy I thought I would hate for taking my room away from me. Right now as I look at him knelt down, touching the skin of the water with his fingertips, I am grateful. Grateful that I've found him. Grateful that he has looked up and found me.

There is no smile on his face. He just bows in acknowledgment. I walk farther down to join him, removing the weight of my backpack, then kneel down next to him. He looks back at the water. My eyes follow. A flash of orange scales catches the rays of sun gleaming through the lacy trees above us. Then another flash, white this time.

Koi. We watch as the fish congregate near us. Carver pokes into his pocket and extracts what look like pebbles. He bends down, sprinkling them into the water. The koi wag their bodies in excitement; their round mouths become tunnels inhaling the food. "So, what, you walk around with fish food in your pocket?" I ask.

"When I come here, I do." An orange koi practically lifts its head out of the water. Carver reaches down and pets it.

"You're petting a fish," I say, shocked.

"Try it." Carver removes his hand from the koi, who goes back underwater and rises to the surface again. I reach over and touch it on its scaly head. The muscles of its body press up toward my hand.

"Pretty great, huh?" Carver asks. And the thought of eating one of these creatures makes me mourn the canned tuna I've eaten throughout my life.

"I'm sorry I couldn't meet you at the corner," I tell him.

"I figured you just backed out," he says, looking down at the fish.

"No, my mom ended up taking me to school and I didn't—"

Carver interrupts. "Don't worry about it. I'm just glad you made it."

"Yeah, me too." I shift from kneeling to sitting. "So you work at a place like this in San Francisco?"

"Yeah. The San Francisco gardens are bigger, though. And the koi there definitely have more dominion over the place than the ones here do." Makes me want dominion over something, too. "The koi live in the moon-viewing garden."

"What's a moon-viewing garden?"

"There're just lots of reflective elements." Carver scatters more feed into the pond. I'm amazed at the fish's courtesy to one another. They aren't squabbling over the food like dogs do. "It's cool. At night, you can see the moon in the pond. The glow of it reflects off the leaves of the Japanese maple trees. You can see all of it reflected in a gazing ball."

"And what's a gazing ball?"

"This huge ball that looks like solid mercury. It's centered in the garden, set on top of a metal stand. Looking at it, you can see a panoramic view of what's behind you."

Our eyes become little gazing balls looking at the panorama of each other.

That he wanted to bring me here, that he knows things I don't know is so appealing it hurts. It's like there's a whole other world wrapped up in this person, and I want to learn it, to know it, to kiss it. I lean toward Carver in an attempt to try.

Purposeful, controlled attention allows a dog to flourish. —Michael Kaplan, *The Manifesto of Dog*

I feel different when I get to work, like there's more to know, and because of that, the world seems bigger than it did before. The sacrifice of not going to school today was worth the experience of hollyhocks and morning glories. (Carver knows the names of flowers.)

Carver arrives a half hour later, as planned. We go about our day with the secret of our trip between us. A few hours later, I slip a note into the kibble bin that reads "Thanks."

Restriction doesn't feel as bad later that night in my room. It's like I have a gazing ball in my head reflecting my time with Carver this morning. And it feels like enough right now.

On Wednesday morning, Kirby is at the stop sign

first. "What's up?" he says from his position on the ground. "I hate this restriction thing, by the way. I don't even get to talk to you anymore."

"I hate it, too. Won't be joining you for soup night tonight, that's for sure. It's like I've got my own private Alcatraz. I did manage to escape for a little while yesterday."

"Yeah, what are the details of that, by the way? Your text came across very secret agent."

"I went to the botanical gardens with Carver."

"Does your mom know?" Kirby's eyebrows lift.

"Of course, I told her about the whole thing. She's delighted."

"You don't have to get all sarcastic on me."

"Why would you ask me that, you dork? Of course I didn't tell her." I kick the toe of Kirby's high-top and sit down next to him. "I'm taking you there sometime, Kirb. You'd love it. There's a koi pond, a zillion kinds of trees and flowers, and the best thing of all is this huge waterfall. Did you know there was a waterfall, the kind you'd see in the tropics, in our own backyard?"

"Plants? Fish? Since when are you interested in something that doesn't drool or have fur?" he asks. "I'm surprised you ditched school."

"You have a problem with that?" My defenses are going up again.

"If you're gonna start building up a criminal record, I do," he says.

213

"Sounds like a double standard." I spot Nina in the distance. "Why is it okay for Nina to do what she wants, but you expect me to restrain myself?"

"It's not that I expect that. You always restrain yourself, Natalie."

"People change," I say, standing up.

Kirby stands up. "That's what I'm worried about," he murmurs.

"That is so not fair, Kirby." I briskly walk away from him toward Nina.

Fortunately, she delights in my retelling of my morning with Carver and my courage to skip class for such a noble pursuit.

During class, Mr. Klinefelter asks our cooperative groups to review Woodrow Wilson's fourteen points for world peace, 1918, and condense each point into one sentence.

Allison bites her polished black thumbnail while Richard and Laney argue over how to translate "economic barriers." Richard wants "monetary hurdles" while Laney rallies for "financial stumbling blocks."

I try my hand at mediation. "Mr. Klinefelter didn't say we had to change the wording. Let's just keep that phrase so we can get through this."

"What do you care?" Laney says. "You're just going to go along with what we choose, anyway."

"What's that supposed to mean?" My heart skips ten beats.

"Nothing." Laney shrugs it off.

"No, really, Laney," I say forcefully, "I want to know what you mean." Allison and Richard look at me as if I'm birthing a baby out of my head.

"I said, nothing," growls Laney.

"Well, it sort of felt like something." It's out. I have to keep going, push. Deep breath, blood rushing to face, keep back tears. "It's fine that Nina wants to be friends with you; that doesn't bother me. And it doesn't bother me that you like Carver. But you can stop trying to make me feel like a useless piece of crap, because I'm not. So let's just say 'economic barriers' and move on to Wilson's fourth point."

" 'Removing economic barriers' it is!" says Richard, excitedly scribbling it down on a piece of paper. Allison cracks her knuckles. Laney stares at me.

I stare back this time. Laney shrugs again, and for the first time in my entire universe involving Laney Benning, I feel something akin to strength. It feels good.

After class I take my note to the attendance office. Having covered that base, I strut—yes, strut—toward the vending machines to treat Kirby, Nina, and myself to CornNuts. I don't mention my interaction with Laney to them, but I feel great just knowing that I stood up for myself.

Mom doesn't even call me on my barking cell before work. It is a good day!

When I get to the clinic, Luther, a bulldog with several chins and broad sloping shoulders, is there, looking like a gargoyle keeping guard. It's hard to take him seriously, though, because his tongue is unable to fit in his mouth. Mrs. Bradford, his owner, says hello as I walk into the reception area.

The phone rings after I settle into my chair. "Dr. Kaplan's office."

"I need to talk to you," Mom says, no inflection of emotion in her voice.

"Okay," I answer, "I'll be right there." My stomach drops as I walk into Mom's office.

Mom sits behind her desk, her hands folded on top. I know from this body language that she is mad. I sit down in the vinyl seat across from her.

Mom purses her lips and releases a gigantoid sigh. "How do you spell 'excuse'?" she asks me.

Play dead. Do a little perk-of-the-ears doggie head tilt. Something. I play stupid. "Why?"

"Because you spelled it wrong on the note you forged for the attendance office. You left out the *c*."

Stupid handwriting! Need spell check! "So you're mad about me misspelling a word?" I ask.

"Don't be a s-m-a-r-t a-s-s," Mom says sourly. "Explain this to me, Natalie, because I don't understand why you would voluntarily take a class over the summer and, behind my back, skip school." Mom makes a noise in her throat as if she is going to spit fire.

All the leafy green lushness of the botanical gardens, along with the cheery flowers, wilts in fast-forward motion. Is it possible that there is some God of Truth hovering over me full-time? Why can't I get away with anything? Can I do one measly thing without my mother getting involved?

I take a deep breath, remember the image of me with Laney today. "I went to the botanical gardens," I announce.

"You went with Carver."

"Yes."

"So you skipped school and went behind my back to be with Carver?"

"I was at school for a little while," I say, trying to convince her that I didn't completely miss it, that I didn't run away mischievously as she left the parking lot yesterday. "But I didn't go to spite you. I went because I wanted to go. Asking permission wasn't really an option because I knew you wouldn't let me." Although I'm afraid for myself right now, I am more concerned about Carver. I don't want him to get sent home.

I add, "It's not Carver's fault."

"What is going on with you?" Mom's voice rises twelve octaves. "Why are you doing this?" The same spiel I got from Kirby.

"Really, Mom, it's no big deal. We were at the botanical gardens, not a bar or a hotel room."

"It might be better for you to start thinking about what you did do instead of what you didn't do, Natalie. Take some responsibility, won't you?" She

217

leans over her desk toward me, her jaw clenched. "And don't you dare blame me, either."

Worthless tears crawl down my face again. Mom casts her eyes away from me. "I'm taking you to school from now on."

Fine. Tighten the grip. Put me in a box. I'm going to find a way out.

Mom gets up from her desk and walks toward the door.

She wants me to act responsibly yet not make my own decisions? Before Mom walks out the door, I need to say it, even though I have to blubber it through my tears: "I could do so much worse, Mom."

Mom turns. "Yeah, well, you could do much better."

I snortle in a drip from my nose. She gets the last word, because she is out the door.

I kick the ground, stand up and punch the air, then crumple into a ball on the vinyl chair and cry.

I can't keep trying to live up to these impossible standards of hers. Good grades didn't please her. Being compliant didn't get me anywhere, either. I'm damned if I do or don't.

There are no notes in the kibble bin that afternoon, no quick sneaks from Carver to my desk when Mom is in the exam room. She's definitely had a talk with him. He's laying low and I vow to rub Fu-Fu all night in hopes that Mom will not send him home.

Thursday morning. Mom punches the car into reverse and we pick up Nina and Kirby at the corner. They sit in the backseat, probably sensing the tension between Mom and me, because they remain unusually quiet.

At school Mom parks the car. "You can just drop us off," I say.

"No, I'll walk with you." She pulls her keys from the ignition and follows us out of the car. Nina and Kirby stay on either side of me, protecting me from Mom, who keeps a close clip behind us. She follows us all the way to the classroom door.

Mom stands in the doorway until I am seated in my desk. I glare at her and she walks away.

One time I read a true story about this kid in Russia who was abandoned by his parents. He lived on the streets among stray dogs. Later, when he was taken into custody by social workers, he told them he was better off living with the dogs than with his parents because the dogs at least made him feel loved and protected.

Mom is not making me feel loved and protected. On the contrary: I'm feeling doubted and suffocated. I probably would've been better off raised by dogs.

Following rules is mental stimulation for a dog.

—Michael Kaplan, *The Manifesto of Dog*

It's amazing what one can accomplish on an index card.

A 3 x 5 card, specifically. After I spend a few hours in my room on Thursday night flipping through terms and definitions for tomorrow's test, I realize I am able to write my first name ninety times on one side of an index card. I write the word "hell" on the other side. There's room for 135 hells.

I don't dare say I am in a living hell. Living hell is the poop-covered, blood-encrusted grounds where millions of dogs in China are forced to live until they meet their cruel fate of being slowly slaughtered for food or for their fur. Living hell is what Grandma experienced in the Holocaust. My problems are thin and wimpy compared with true suffering. But dog or human, no one likes to feel trapped.

I write the word "escape" on a new index card. Back and front, the card holds 188 "escapes."

Around ten-thirty p.m., an hour after the house assumes darkness, I slip on a pair of many-pocketed cargo pants that generously accommodate my index cards. I rub Fu-Fu, and the dogs follow me downstairs, where I grab three leashes from the entry hall. The dogs' bodies flail about in excitement as I reach for them. We head out the front door and up the stairs leading to the room above the garage.

Light seeps through the windows, but there is no answer after I knock. This is proof that life goes on without me. Where is Carver, anyway? How could I not have noticed him leaving the room? Standing on the landing outside his door, I look down at Laney's porch. Nina was supposed to go to the movies with Laney tonight.

Instead of going back into the house, the dogs and I venture out a few blocks, to Kirby's place. I am just walking the dogs; Mom can't blame me for that.

Kirby answers the door. He looks at the dogs, whose noses are attacking the hedge lining the front porch. "That's Paco's favorite pee spot," he says, explaining the sniffing frenzy. "So what are you doing here? I thought you were on restriction."

"I'm taking the dogs for a walk," I say.

"It's sort of late for that, don't you think?"

"Maybe I'm rebelling at the same time."

"You're such a hell-raiser, aren't you?" Kirby makes a fake microphone with his fist. "Girl rebels by taking her dogs for a walk. . . . News at eleven."

I laugh.

Kirby crosses his arms and leans against the door-frame. "I'm not so sure I want to be linked to your rebellious ways. I will top your mom's shit list if she finds you here."

"First, the woman sleeps like a log. Second, if you want me to leave, just say so."

Kirby eases onto the porch, scanning the empty sidewalk for signs of my mom. "Okay, y'all can come in. My mom is out playing bunco, anyway."

I walk in and we settle at the kitchen table; the dogs wander around the house, sniffing the afterglow of Paco. "Where're Paco and Bogart?" I ask.

"Paco's with my mom. As for Bogart, it's turned into a shared-custody thing." Kirby fills two glasses with orange juice from the fridge. "He's here one night, found the next day, spends a night with the ruthless owners, and comes on back. Maryann's parents have done nothing to secure their yard."

"I told you a long time ago that you should read *Shiloh*. Had you read it, you would clearly see that Bogart is your Shiloh."

"I'll add it to my summer reading list." He sets a

glass down in front of me and nabs a box of ginger-snaps from the pantry.

"Thanks," I say, raising my glass to him.

Kirby joins me at the table. "So are you going to tell me what you're doing out of the house?"

With a mouthful of gingersnap, I pull an index card out of my side pocket. Kirby reads it. "Escape? Looks like you wrote it a lot."

"I am tired of being good and getting no credit for it. Why not rise to the occasion and be the rabble-rouser my mom thinks I am? I want some adventure."

"You don't get enough adventure with Carver?" He swills his orange juice.

I stop midswig of mine. "We're not discussing this again."

"Fine." Kirby leans back into his chair and pushes his glasses up higher on the bridge of his nose.

"Look, I'm here to visit. I miss you and we need to make nice, since we've been quibbling a lot lately." The dogs come into the kitchen and vie for a position at Paco's tiny food and water dishes. "Sorry," I say. "These dogs have bottomless pits for stomachs."

"No big deal." He shrugs.

"Let's do something daring."

"Not going to jump off the roof if that's what you have in mind."

I look toward the box of wine on top of the refrigerator and point to it. "What about that?"

Kirby finds what I'm looking at. "That has been

there for like three years. My mom doesn't drink pink wine. Only red."

"So your mom won't know if there's some missing?" I arch my eyebrows at him.

"Probably not." He widens his eyes. "Why, you want a drink?"

"Yes, I do. You know I've never really let myself indulge and I may as well do it with someone I trust."

"Okay, maybe I should be honored, but there's no way I'm going to be responsible for your first hangover. Did you not see Laney the other night?"

"It's obvious she overdid it. We don't have to drink that much, Kirb. Just a little. Just enough to feel like we're outside of ourselves. Please?"

"No. You can be mad at me, but no. Besides, we have a test tomorrow." He's worse than I am.

I reach over to him. "We'll drink slowly. We can quiz each other on potential test questions while we're drinking. C'mon. We're safe. We're not driving. Your mom plays bunco until dawn. We can add water or something to the box so that if she lifts it, it won't be lighter. In case she checks on those types of things. She hasn't touched it, right?"

Kirby shakes his head.

"Please?" I beg.

Kirby looks from me to the box of wine. "At least you're polite about it."

We go into the bathroom and weigh the wine box, because neither of us knows how to convert the five liters of wine to pounds. We decide that this would make a fantastic word problem in a math textbook should we ever author one.

We find a medicine syringe of Paco's, clean it, and figure out how to insert water into the spigot to make up for the emptied contents. Our asses are completely covered.

Back in the kitchen, Kirby rinses out our glasses. I'm thrilled that we are going to do something we're forbidden to do. I don't have Mom's permission. I'm not stealing from Mom's wine reserves. This belongs to me.

Kirby fills the small glasses with about a tablespoon of pink wine. "Are you kidding?" I ask. "That might be adequate for an amoeba, but not me. Fill it up more. Please."

"Yes, Miss Manners."

The first sips are the most difficult. We even plug our noses while we sip, because the wine is bitter, probably expired...if wine expires. Is it wine or cheese that ages? Whatever wine does, it's hard to believe people actually like the taste of it.

Forty-some minutes later, we are sitting cross-legged in Kirby's backyard with a bag of stale trail mix and our second empty glass of wine. The current weight of the wine box on top of the fridge is 11.2 pounds, so the syringe method is working.

The dogs are lumped between us, sleeping. Party poopers.

Kirby runs into the house to fill another glass. I

know I've had enough, because I'm warm, sort of fuzzy. The sound of a train rumbling over tracks in the distance is more audible. The air smells saltier. I feel like someone is pushing me ever so slightly on a swing.

Kirby returns with more of his wine. We lie back on the grass in the center of the backyard, looking at the dark sky mottled with stars. "I'm gonna learn the stars," says Kirby. "Ever notice how in movies and books and stuff, stars are so important? Like people can read the stars as if they're an alphabet and it sets the mood for romance or some sort of epiphany. I'm totally illiterate. I couldn't even point in the direction of the Big Dipper."

"Yeah." I sigh.

"I bet Crater's the kind of guy who knows the stars."

"Carver, you mean?"

"Whatever. I bet he has a cheat sheet of the constellations in his pocket so he can sound all romantic about the stars when he's with a girl."

I prop myself up on the backs of my elbows. "Oh, so you think he's been with a lot of other girls?"

"Definitely." He puts his hands behind his head and crosses one foot over the other.

"Thanks a lot, Kirb." I get up feeling like I'm on an elevator, so I put my arms out like wings for some balance. The dogs lazily raise their heads.

"Great." Kirby stands, downs the rest of his wine, throws the glass on the lawn, raises his arms, and screams, "Zip and Go! Wallet!"

"What?" I ask, steadying myself as I straighten up. "Kirby, maybe you should go lie down. You've probably had more than you should."

"Yep! Zip and Go! Wallet," Kirby says, shooting an arm up toward the sky like a rocket.

"Kirby, I don't get what you are saying. You're not making sense."

"Oh, I'm making perfect sense." He looks at me and flies into storytelling mode. "I was eight, eating my Crazy-Os cereal. The back of the cereal box offered the Zip and Go! Wallet, free with three proofs of purchase. So I ate Crazy-Os at every meal for an entire week, got my little proof-of-purchase things, smashed my piggy bank open for shipping and handling fees, and sent in my labels." He rests his hands on top of his head.

"Okay." I can't figure out where he is going with this.

"And you know what?" Kirby lets his arms dangle to his sides. "That stupid thing never showed up in the mail." He stops talking and looks beyond me, toward the stars, until I have to take a look, too. "It's like all the days I've saved on you, Natalie. Seeing you with Carver feels the same as having spent time being excited about that wallet, a waste for something that never even bothered to show up. You're my Zip and Go! Wallet."

"But Kirby, I am here. You're not alone." I step in closer to him.

"Natalie, you don't understand." He looks from the sky to me. "I like you."

Shit.

"Kirby, you're drunk. You should go to sleep."

"I've liked you for a long time. Probably ever since our first cross-country lap together."

I've had too much wine, because this is playing out like some never-supposed-to-happen blooper from the filmstrip in my head that has been locked away. Am I hallucinating, or do all people just talk crazy talk when they drink?

"Kirby? We're friends. I'd never want to jeopardize that. Ever." He looks at me. Long. Hard. "No." I shake my head. "Friends who hook up end up breaking up. And from there, you can't turn back and just be friends. We can't, Kirby. Friends. Friends only."

"Friends only. Right," he says, wagging a finger at me. "Good comeback." He limps toward the house. "I'll take you home."

The walk back to my house is long. It feels as though the short blocks are sprawling cornfields that take forever to go across. I wonder if I'd be able to move without the dogs leading me on their leashes.

Kirby and I don't say a word to each other; it feels strange. Kirby tells me he likes me, and *wham!* we are not who we were a few hours ago.

My house is still pitch-black when we approach; even the room above the garage seems vacant and asleep. Kirby looks at me when I stop at the front walkway. "See ya," he says. His shoulders sag as he traces his steps back to his house.

I watch until he disappears, feeling more scared than drunk. Because life without Kirby would be like a sky without stars.

Right or wrong, dog shows are a blatant display of submission.

—Michael Kaplan, *The Manifesto of Dog*

On Friday morning my alarm beeps in unison with the throbbing of my head. Wine. Blech. Now I can say I've been sort of drunk, but all I have to show for it is what feels like a brain hemorrhage and an injured friendship.

When I sit up, my head feels inside out. If I could smell the taste in my mouth, I'd probably throw up.

Without permission, I grab the phone. I call Kirby so that I'll know we're okay. I don't want him to feel weird when we pick him up at the corner. There is no answer on his home phone. I try his cell. No answer. He always answers his cell, even if he has to step out of the shower with a dripping body. He's avoiding me.

I reach for last night's cargo pants and rifle around

for the index cards. I want to see if I've lost memory of what I studied for today's test.

I haven't lost it, but it sure is harder to retrieve. That could be partly because of my wondering where Carver was last night and my hoping that I haven't lost Kirby.

There is a surge of remorse accompanying the headache and the wondering and the worry. Mom wasn't waiting for me when I came through the door last night. I actually got away with something. Big relief, yes, but she trusted that I was in my room, respecting her terms of restriction.

I will not feel bad about this. I will not.

When we pick Nina up at the stop sign, she informs me that Kirby is driving himself to school. "He's got to do a pickup for his mom right after class," she says. He's lying. He drove so he could avoid me.

After Mom drops us off and we make it into the classroom, there is no sign of Kirby. Open seats next to Laney and Maryann force us in their direction. I save a seat for Kirby and figure that if I can drink wine from a box, I can certainly sit near Nina's friends as they reminisce about Orlando Bloom's performance in last night's movie.

When class starts, Kirby rushes in and sits in the empty seat closest to the door, not the one I saved for him. Mr. Klinefelter fills the first few hours with lecture and we have the remaining time to complete our tests, after which we are allowed to leave.

Kirby is the first one to finish his test. He rushes out the door once he plops it on Mr. Klinefelter's desk. I, however, am the last student to leave class, taking extra time to answer the test questions. My brain feels slowed. The information is there, but it's not high speed; this is more like sitting in rush-hour traffic than cruising in the carpool lane, a pleasure I've personally been denied, since I am not allowed to drive on the freeway.

Mom calls as I exit the classroom. I tell her I'm on my way. Heigh-ho. Heigh-ho.

When I walk outside into the quad, Carver is there. Pixie arrives sort of sluggishly, but she manages to do a balance beam routine along the arteries leading from my heart. Nina, Maryann, and Laney stand around him. "Let's get something to eat," Nina says when I approach, pulling Laney and Maryann toward the vending area, giving me space alone with him.

"What're you doing here?" I ask.

He leans in and pecks me on the cheek. "I'm on my lunch hour and wanted to know if you'd like to hang out tonight," he says.

"Sounds great, but I'm grounded, remember?"

"Ah, yes, but I've found a way to get past that irritating detail."

I'm not sure I have any rebellion left in me right now unless it means ripping the Do Not Remove tags off my mattress. "I'm listening."

"I'll go with you tonight when you take your grandma to rummy."

"You've done your research. I do have to drive her, but I'm pretty sure my mom will not let you go with me in the car. We're not supposed to be alone together, remember?"

"Well, technically, we won't be alone. Your grandma will be with us. I'm going to hide in the backseat." He taps his temple with his finger. "Pretty smart, eh? We can hang out in the car while you wait for your grandma in the parking lot."

I run my thumb over the soft bristles of hair on his chin. I've missed being near him the past few days. "But when my grandma is inside the senior center, we'll be alone."

"Not really." Carver places his hands on my waist and eases me closer to him. "We're never really alone, right? I mean, there's a whole universe surrounding us."

Pixie has suddenly gone into an Olympic-style floor routine. I can even feel the warmth flowing into my breasts. "If my mom found out, she'd have a seizure. I'm sure she'd send you home."

Carver drops a kiss on my neck. "I am home." My goose bumps get goose bumps, and Miss Pixie slides into the labyrinth of my large intestine with a *wheeee!*

I know I shouldn't, but I whisper into the curl of Carver's ear, "Yes."

On my way to work, I walk by Rescued Threads, where Kirby's Civic is parked out front. I risk being late because this is warranted and worth any harm that may come to me.

Paco meets me at the entrance of the store. He's so small that wagging his tail causes his entire puffball body to lash about in one big excited convulsion. "Hey, Paco." I give him my palm and let my fingers hide inside the thick fur behind his ear, giving him a good scratch.

Eve is helping a redheaded woman decide between a red toile sundress and an orange one with a totem pole print. She waves when she sees me. "Which one do you think, Nattie?" she asks.

"Totem pole, definitely." Redheaded woman props her chin in her hand and quizzically ping-pongs between the two dresses. She's not convinced.

"Thanks for your fashion advice!" Eve says. "Kirby's in the back." Paco trots over to Eve.

I walk through the velvet curtain and find Kirby sitting on the floor amid little plastic bags of screws, assembling what looks like the beginning of a hat rack. A diagram splays out in front of him. Surrounding him are lumps of clothes that are ready to be tagged and sold.

"Missed you at school today," I say. I sit down on the ground next to him. "You rushed out of there so fast, I didn't get a chance to talk to you."

Kirby's blue hair has faded; his boyish features are on the brink of manhood. If I could have told the gawky seventh-grade version of him that in a few years he'd be handsome, he'd never have believed me.

"Are you mad at me?" I ask. Kirby loosely bends his knees up toward his chest and rests his arms on them.

"Truth?"

I nod.

"A little." He points a finger at me. "It's your fault for fixating on that stupid box of wine." Covering his face with his hands, he says, "I just feel like an ass. You know how I feel about you now and the feeling isn't mutual. I'm the loser, the pathetic one who can't get the girl."

I peel his hands away from his face and hold on to them. "You so have the girl, Kirby. Don't tell Nina and, please, don't let my dogs know, because if they ever find out, they'll punish me by peeing in my closet, but you, Kirby, are the best." He jerks his head back a bit as if he's been shaken.

"Really," I continue. "You're the best thing, person, and friend in my life. I don't know how to say this without sounding utterly cliché, but I can't risk losing you." I let his hands go. "Let's just say, for example, we kiss."

"Really?" he says, looking hopeful.

"No, not really. I'm speaking hypothetically here. Get your head out of the gutter."

"Give me a second, then." He pauses as if he's running live camera shots through his head. "Okay, I'm ready."

"Let's say we kiss. And that kiss leads to a relationship. And that relationship leads to the inevitable breakup. How do we go back to what we've had?" Kirby starts to answer, but I stop him. "We can't go back. It's like neutering a dog. You can't put all those parts back into place once they've been sucked out."

"Thanks for the visual. But I disagree. It's not like a neutered dog, Natalie. Neutered dogs still hump legs."

"Okay, wrong analogy, then. I just know that things will change between us, and I'm not willing to go there. I don't want to risk our friendship. Not now."

"So what are you saying? Someday?"

"No. I can't see into the future. I just know that, now, I want exactly what we have."

Kirby picks up some stray screws from the floor and lets them roll around in the cup of his hand. "I still feel like an ass."

"Well, don't." I take his hand in mine and give it a squeeze. "You and me? We're gonna be fine."

"Ruh?" Kirby asks in his Scooby voice.

"Promise." I give him my warmest smile. "We're even gonna go on eBay and find you a Zip and Go! Wallet."

* * *

236

I get to work about ten minutes late, but Mom is occupied in the exam room. Convenient timing and very much needed.

Things with Kirby feel more straightened out. Even though we may be on different pages, knowing where we are prevents us from losing each other.

It could be I've approached this lie thing in the wrong way. Instead of looking at the deposit slip of seasonal lies, I spend the rest of the afternoon pretending that sixteen years of good behavior amounts to something. Like there's a bank account where I've deposited good in order to withdraw some cold, hard bad. I deposit more today by being polite to my mom and giving her more than monosyllabic answers to her questions.

In the late afternoon, my nerves are bundled in doubt. I leave a note in the kibble bin for Carver. "I can't do it."

I retrieve a note from him later. "You can. Don't worry."

Carver leaves work at five p.m. and gives me a wink on his way out. He'll be back here by five-fifty to sneak into the unlocked car.

Diana, a large fluffy-haired white Samoyed, leads her short and portly owner, Mrs. Gonzales, through the front door of the clinic at 5:48 p.m. Mrs. Gonzales' thick black hair is disheveled, and sweat glosses her face. It looks like Diana has dragged her, Iditarod-style, for several blocks.

Mom comes out of the exam room with Madame Bovary, a small, elderly, white-muzzled Boston terrier, and her owner. Diana jumps playfully at Madame Bovary, who lowers her head and fiercely snarls in reaction. She's obviously not feeling well, because Boston terriers normally have a gentle disposition.

Mom interferes and tells Mrs. Gonzales and Diana to wait in the exam room. Looking relieved, Madame Bovary and her owner wait for me to tally the bill.

Mom leans over the reception counter. "You should go get your grandmother soon."

"Sure," I say. A pang of guilt. Ignore it. Ignore it.

She stares at my strand of dyed hair for a minute. "Your blue is fading."

"Yeah." I nod. "Good thing, huh?"

"Drive safely," she says. "And wait for her in the parking lot."

I nod. Mom thinks I'm being a good sport about being on restriction. At least Madame Bovary, the Boston terrier, made her discontent apparent when Diana provoked her. The best I can do is behave like a hedonistic pathological liar living an alternate life.

Speaking of an alternate life, Carver is probably sneaking into the car right about now.

It behooves an owner to know that a dog, in essence, is unpredictable.

—Michael Kaplan, *The Manifesto of Dog*

"You there?" I ask when I get into the driver's seat.

"Of course," Carver answers in a muffled voice. I look behind me, into the backseat, where a huge duffel bag lies on the ground next to Carver (who appears to be a hump covered by a plaid flannel blanket).

"What's with the humongous bag?"

Carver peeks out from the blanket, his hair feathery with static electricity. "Provisions. That's all you get to know." For a second, Pixie holds up a flashing yellow warning light. I want to ask him more about the contents of the bag, but I know I'm prone to fits of paranoia. He wouldn't do anything too risky after the whole pot episode. No way.

I take a deep breath, start the car, and force that

stupid scared voice of mine out of my head. I feel Carver pushing into the back of my seat. "Carver?"

"Hmm?"

"You're not wearing a seat belt."

"No, but I'm not going to fly out of the car if you hit something." He sounds like he's talking from inside a cave. "You're not planning on hitting anything, are you?"

"No." I squeeze into highway traffic and am cut off by a red pickup truck and forced to pound on the brakes.

Carver pops out from beneath his blanket again. "Okay, so maybe I do need a seat belt."

It's past six. When we get to the railroad crossing, the giant black-and-white-striped arms are lowered. The world always slows down when I'm in a hurry!

A freight train crawls along the tracks. The worry about Carver being in the backseat closes in on me like it never really left. I keep hearing Mom say we're not supposed to be alone together, and even though the "universe" surrounds us, I'm starting to think that I'm doing the wrong thing.

"Carver?"

"Yes?"

"What if I get pulled over by the cops?"

"You don't drive fast enough to do that," he says. I'm slightly offended. "Besides"—he comes out from beneath the blanket and is so close to me I can feel his breath—"if you're always asking 'what if,' you'd never leave the house."

I look at him in the rearview mirror. "I know, but I could lose my license if I'm caught, because you're not wearing your seat belt. My mom would find out and she'd yank away yet another privilege. I barely get to drive as it is."

Carver lets out a huge sigh, running his hand through his flyaway hair. "You can think of the worst-case scenario for any situation. You could stop crossing the street because you might get hit by a car. You might stop getting out of bed if you thought about getting struck by lightning or having a tree freakishly topple onto you."

"Carver, I'm a victim of worst-case scenarios, if you haven't noticed. My mom found us in bed together, she found out I skipped school. Doesn't it follow that this will lead me to another worst-case scenario?"

"No, you see, you've had your share. This is your freebie," he says. "Don't worry, okay? You'll see, it'll actually be fun."

The gates in front of the train tracks rise. I drive through the crossing and toward home. Carver resumes hiding under his blanket.

Grandma is tapping her white-patent-leather-clad foot on the curb when we get there. I jump out of the car and run to her side to open the door for her. "I can do it," she says. "You are late." She kisses my cheek.

"Sorry," I say. From Grandma's viewpoint outside, Carver cannot be seen in the backseat.

Once the two of us are buckled in, I drive down the block, toward the stop sign. "Reva's daughter is getting divorced," she says. "That vay!" She points in the direction we're driving.

"Why?" I try to keep my cool and pretend that there's not another passenger in the backseat.

"Her husband is not very attentive."

At the stop sign, a police car drives by in the opposite direction. Panic. "A cop," I blurt.

"No, Reva's husband is not a policeman. He is a lawyer," Grandma says, continuing our conversation.

"He's turning around," I say. I see the cop in my side-view mirror as I sit stunned at the stop sign.

"Just go," Carver says in a loud whisper.

"Who is saying that?" Grandma is startled and looks around the cabin of the car.

"I'm pulling over!" I shout. I steer the car to the curb. The cop passes me. "You have to get out of the car. I can't do this."

"Vhat? Vhy?" Grandma looks at me with her eyes narrowed. "Vhat is going on?"

"No, I mean you, Carver." I look straight ahead and watch the police car fade into the length of the never-ending street.

"Why? Are you being pulled over?" Carver asks, still under his blanket.

"Carver is back there?" Grandma yells, craning her neck toward the backseat.

"Please, Carver, I can't do it." Carver comes out from behind the blanket.

"Vhat are you doing here?" Grandma waits for him to answer.

I pounce in before he can say anything. "I'm sorry, Grandma. Give me a minute."

I step out of the car and Carver follows me to the sidewalk. We stand underneath a leafless tree. I gauge a rise in Carver's frustration level: red floods his cheeks. "You are great, Carver. Fun. Spontaneous. I just—" Oh, no, tears. Look down! Wipe them away! I look at a crack in the sidewalk. "I just can't do this. It doesn't feel right."

How can this not feel right? There's a wonderful guy standing in front of me who makes me want to vampire-kiss right into his neck, but I'm too worried to go forward with this. I must be a freak.

Grandma is watching us from inside the car.

I can feel Carver look at me. Perhaps he's trying to define me. "Not everything you do is going to lead to the worst possible consequence." He must think I'm a slow learner, because he told me this in the car about five minutes ago. I hear the words, but I can't seem to understand their meaning. There is always a consequence.

He allows me some time to study the sidewalk crack

a little longer. When I look up at his green eyes, he shakes his head. And with that, he walks back toward home. For the first time in the weeks that I've known him, his shoulders slump. He doesn't look back at me. I stay on the sidewalk, ignoring Grandma's ring-fingered tapping on the window.

I want Carver to know me better. If he did, he'd know that I've lied to my mom, ditched school, prowled out of the house, and consumed alcohol—all within a week. If he knew these were all firsts for me, maybe he'd give me a break or at least understand why his hiding in the car was just a little too much to bear.

My face is wet with tears when I get back into the car. "Please don't say anything to Mom, Grandma. He's out of the car, okay? It was a mistake."

I expect Grandma's head to spin 360 degrees while she says, "I'm late!" but instead, she looks at me and asks, "Vhat is vrong?"

I hang my arms over the steering wheel and rest my head on it. "I'm tired of being good."

"Hiding a boy in the car is being good?"

"But I made him get out."

"That is because you are an honest girl," she says proudly.

Tears wet the steering wheel and I wonder if they're heavy enough to sound the horn. "No," I heave, "I'm not an honest girl. I've been lying to Mom."

"But you do not do it vell. It stays vith you"—she

reaches over and gently touches my stomach—"here. You feel bad about it."

"So that makes it right?" I straighten up, trying to compose myself.

"No!" Her petrified pointer finger jabs toward my face. I flinch. "You feel bad because you are not being true to yourself." She slaps her hand on the dashboard. "And vhen you are not true to self, that is the biggest lie of all, vhen you lie to yourself."

"Grandma?" I ask.

"Vhat?"

"Was Mom true to herself when she was my age?"

Grandma takes a deep breath and looks out the window. "Your mother always had a drive inside. She always had her nose in a book. Always serious. Your grandpa and I tell her to relax, to smell the roses. But she did not listen. Perhaps that vas her vay of being true to herself."

I try to suppress my crying on the way to the senior center. Out of sympathy, Grandma refrains from screaming driving directions. When we get there, she turns to me. "I can stay vith you," she says.

"Thanks, but a little time alone might do me good," I say. "I'll be here when you're done."

Grandma hesitates, then gets out and walks through the double doors of the senior center.

I climb into the backseat and wrap myself in the plaid blanket. Carver's bag is at my feet. I sniffle, wipe my nose on the blanket, unzip the bulky bag, reach into it, and pull out a large CD player. There're a tapered white candle with holder, matches, two plastic cups, a bottle of sparkling apple cider, and a box from the Crusty Crumb Bakery containing two devil's food chocolate cupcakes.

I press Play on the CD player. Otis Redding's buttery voice spills from the speakers.

> *These arms of mine*
> *They are yearning*
> *Yearning from wanting you.*

I press Stop on the CD player, get in the front seat, and start the car. I've an hour and fifteen minutes to be true to myself.

Genetics, not abandonment, causes a dog to stray. —Michael Kaplan, *The Manifesto of Dog*

I loop back toward the route I took to get to the senior center. Every person I pass, be it potbellied man watering his lawn or slender woman on a porch swing tending to a crossword puzzle, becomes subject to scrutiny. After ten minutes of driving at street-sweeper speed, I am still unable to find who I am searching for.

Carver left his key in the duffel bag, so I know he didn't go home. I decide to follow my intuition to Juniper Street.

Less than halfway down the road, I see Carver sitting under some sort of willowy tree in front of the vacant house where he, Laney, and I trespassed two weeks ago.

I press the brakes once Carver is framed in my window. When he looks up at me, I am trembling inside the car. We are only about fifteen feet from each other, but it feels much farther.

Carver, picture-perfect and simple in his white T-shirt and worn faded jeans, has enough heart in him to muster a smile. It is not the kind of smile that is toothy or ear to ear or sarcastic. It is a soft smile, the kind someone gives you when he recognizes something he's never seen in you; it is a knowing smile.

I steer the car to the opposite side of the street and park. I hoist the duffel bag and the blanket from the backseat and walk across the street to join Carver.

He watches me as I approach, the twitch in his jaw becoming clearer as I get closer. "Here," I say quietly, trying to settle the bag at his feet without letting it make a thud.

Carver looks up at me and shakes his head a little so that the hair almost covering his green eyes sweeps to the side. "Did you peek?" he asks.

"I did." I sit next to him, surprised that he doesn't seem angry with me. "I was tempted to eat the cupcakes."

"Better than their going to waste," he says.

"Carver." I bite my lip. "I'm sorry."

"Yeah, well." He reaches down to pick up a small

jagged rock from the street and tosses it from one hand to the other. "I've never met a person like you, someone who can actually trace all the thoughts that lead up to a no." Is that bad or good? "Maybe you take it too far, though. We were just going to sit in the parking lot of a senior citizen center."

"You're right, but you don't seem to question things the way I do. I wish I could just dive headfirst without having to listen to my overactive conscience." I sigh. "But I don't think I can."

The rock sits in his open palm. For a minute, I think he's going to pet it. "You don't have to be sorry," Carver says. "We're just different."

Does he mean "we're just different" as in "we can't be together"? Or "we're just different" as in "I like you and want to make out with you anyway"?

He is not leaning over for a kiss. I can only assume what he means.

Carver scrapes the rock against the concrete like a piece of chalk. He stops, clutches it in his hand, pulls up his pant leg, and scratches his ankle. There, above his anklebone, is a tattoo. A dragonfly. Not a light, airy-looking one, either. It's a thick-bodied dragonfly, a perfectly rendered one with a matrix of lines and texture running through it.

Mystery solved.

It would have been obvious of him to have a koi etched on his ankle. But koi don't have wings. I'm not exactly sure what the dragonfly represents to him, but right now, I choose to read it as a symbol of freedom.

I pry the rock from his hand and toss it into the street. "You know how to get in there?" I glance over my shoulder at the vacant house behind us.

"Yeah. That's why I'm here." Then it hits me. He's here to meet Laney. "I was going to wait until dark and go into the house."

"With Laney?" I ask.

"No, by myself. But Laney gave me the access code."

"I don't get it," I say. "You have the whole room above the garage to yourself."

He sighs. "I came here last night and even though I didn't feel like I belonged here, I didn't feel like I was intruding."

"You're not intruding, Carver."

"It's obvious your mom thinks I'm not such a good influence on you."

That's it. "Let's go in," I say, standing up.

Carver's eyes widen. "Are you serious?"

"Grab the bag." I have an hour before I have to pick up Grandma.

The pinkening of the sky follows us inside the house. Carver takes my hand and leads me up the stairs into a different room than the one he, Laney, and I went into before. Outside the window of the room, a huge tree with feathery purple blooms stretches out its many branches.

Standing next to the window, we kiss for a long time—long enough for the room to darken another few shades.

After about fifteen minutes of tender kisses, we set up a picnic on the blanket and feed each other moist chocolate cupcakes amid candlelight and Otis Redding.

Carver gets closer to me and rests his head in my lap. My fingers comb through the length of his soft hair. Even though we're not kissing, this is the closest I've felt to him. "Can I ask you something personal?"

"Sure."

"Why did you choose a dragonfly—you know, for your tattoo?"

"Ah, that." He wipes a smear of cupcake from my chin and licks it off his finger. Pixie pirouettes. "I've always thought it was cool how dragonflies could inhabit water and air. Their coloring changes as they reflect and refract light. It's just a cool reminder that we're not stagnant. I don't ever want to become one thing, you know? There're too many possibilities."

I lean down to kiss him and then pull back to glance at my watch: twenty-five minutes left. I should leave in fifteen to be safe. Carver sees me looking at my watch, takes it off my wrist, and places it in the enormous duffel bag. "I won't let you be late." Inspired by the dragonfly, I let the light of Carver's words inside me, trusting him.

We shift to lie on the blanket side by side. The candle flickers, the cider fizzes, and the soulful voice of Otis Redding swells throughout the room. The little dragonfly on Carver's ankle comes to life and soars above us, meeting Pixie somewhere between my heart and my head as Carver and I meld into a kiss.

Tonight, our kissing becomes more urgent, less tidy. We allow our tongues to wet each other's lips. I want to know how it feels for him to touch me. I stopped him the other night, but I am in control and know how far I want to go with him. I reach down to the hem of my T-shirt and wiggle it up over my head. Carver arches back to look at me. His hand reaches inside the worn fabric of my bra and cups my breast, his thumb tracing its roundness.

He leans into me. "You're beautiful, Natalie." He brings his mouth back to mine. His hand stays on the bare warmth of my chest, circling until it freezes because there is a sound.

Noise.

An unexpected drumbeat that becomes a steady *thump, thump, thump* of footsteps echoing up the stairs.

We pull back from each other. I become a panic of movement, searching for my shirt.

"Who is up here?" It's the voice of a man.

I am going to die. Right here. Right now.

Carver leans over and blows out the candle, and the smell of smoke lingers in the room with us like a guilty third person. Unable to find my shirt, I wrap my arms around myself. The doorway frames the tall burly shadows of two police officers.

To a dog, limbo and boredom are excruciating states of being.

—Michael Kaplan, *The Manifesto of Dog*

"Miss Kaplan?" Officer DeMarzo says, aiming the beam of his flashlight at me. He recognizes me because his malamute, Randy, is a regular client at the clinic. Both officer and dog are intimidating. Neither is the kind you would approach to offer a scratch under the chin. The other officer, who looks like a huge English mastiff, scrunched face and all, stands silent with his arms crossed over his chest.

Officer DeMarzo looks at Carver and practically growls. "Who are you?"

"Carver Reed," he answers, gently draping the blanket over my bare shoulders. I sidle into it, pulling it over my chest.

"Follow me," Officer DeMarzo says to us. Panic

curls around every bone in my body. What was I thinking?

"Um, Officer?" I say.

"What?"

"Can you give me a minute?"

"Why?" he asks forcefully. "You want time to hide something?"

"Um, no. I need to find my shirt."

"We'll be waiting downstairs," he says. "Son, you come with me." Carver follows.

I find my wadded-up T-shirt that I tried to fling romantically over my head, and squirm into it.

This is bad. Grandma is going to be waiting for me. What time is it? I don't have my watch! Mom's head will explode if she has to bail me out of jail . . . if she's even willing to bail me out.

I walk down the stairs to the front door and meet Carver and the officers outside on the lawn.

"This is a vacant house," Officer DeMarzo says, tucking his thumbs into his belt loops. "You are trespassing, a violation of penal code 602."

"The door was unlocked," lies Carver.

"Son, if we used that logic, anyone would be entitled to a parked car with keys in the ignition." He shakes his head. "Doesn't work." He furrows his dark bushy unibrow and says, "Come with me." We follow him toward the police car. Officer Mastiff walks behind us. My mother is going to chain me to my bed when she finds out about this. And what if she finds out I was topless?

We're ushered into the backseat of the police car. There are no handles on the doors to allow escape—not that we would. Something like chicken wire separates the backseat from the front. We're caged in.

Officer Mastiff stays with us in the cop car while Officer DeMarzo goes inside the house. Checking for contraband, I assume.

"What are we going to do?" I whisper to Carver, looking straight ahead.

"Just stay calm," Carver whispers back. He seems composed, like there's no need to panic.

And there is need to panic.

I am panicking! It is completely appropriate for me to panic, because we are in a police car! My grandmother will be waiting for me! My mom is going to kill me!

"What's the penalty for trespassing?" I ask. Neither Officer Mastiff nor Carver answers. Maybe because trespassing is a one-way ticket into prison! Oh my God! I'll have to go to prison. I'll be behind in school. Wait, I'll probably be expelled from school and forced to go to reform school or something when I get out of prison. "I can't believe this is happening."

"Quiet back there!" Officer Mastiff barks.

Officer DeMarzo comes out of the house with the ginormous duffel bag. He throws it into the trunk, gets into the car, and puts on his seat belt. I don't think

I'm blinking. One cannot panic and blink at the same time.

I don't know what's worse, making Grandma wait at the senior center or being taken in to the police station to be sentenced to prison. I think I'm hyperventilating. Breathe. Breathe. Breathe. "Officer De-Marzo?" I sound croaky.

"What?" he asks as he scribbles something down on a clipboard.

"I'm supposed to pick up my grandmother right now at the senior center. My mom doesn't have the car to pick her up."

Carver reaches over and places his hand on my knee. *It's okay,* he mouths.

We arrive in the parking lot of the senior center before Grandma even comes out. Despite some lawbreaking, I'm early for once. When Grandma shuffles out the doors and into the parking lot, Officer DeMarzo gets out and helps her into the passenger seat, forcing Officer Mastiff to scrunch into the backseat with us. Carver removes his hand from my knee.

As we drive, Grandma asks Officer DeMarzo if he's read us our rights.

"We only do that if we have to question the detained, ma'am," he answers. "There's no need to question these two in the back. They were clearly trespassing."

"My granddaughter is an honest girl!" Grandma says. Obviously, she has a distorted view of me.

Officer DeMarzo pulls into the parking lot of the

police station and leads us into a hallway with about a hundred light fixtures, each bulb weighing in at a blinding one thousand watts. Grandma and Officer DeMarzo walk into one room while Officer Mastiff leads me and Carver to another disturbingly bright room, furnished with a bench seat the length of a crosswalk.

With each hand, Officer Mastiff points to opposite ends of the bench. "There and there," he says. Carver sits at the end closest to the door; I sit at the other end. "No talking." This must be the anticonspiracy room. No one would dare whisper, let alone conspire, with Officer Mastiff keeping watch.

I think I could actually pee in my pants, I'm so scared.

Officer DeMarzo arrives and calls Carver out of the room. Carver turns back to me as he leaves, and he no longer looks calm but instead shuffles out like he's going to be struck with a cattle prod. Officer Mastiff remains in the room, standing in front with his arms crossed. As if I'm a threat.

Finally, enough time has passed for me to accept my possible prison term for what it may be: an opportunity to regroup. Jazz musician John Coltrane got his life together after being in drug rehab, and rehab is probably even worse than prison because you're overcoming an addiction and you're confined. I'll just be confined. Coltrane got out of rehab and went on to rise to the top of his art, becoming the most imitated jazz saxophonist known to date. Grandma can testify to this, since together we witnessed it on A&E's *Biography*.

If there was hope for Coltrane, there has to be hope for me, right? I mean, I don't even have a drug problem. I may need to start playing an instrument, but I'll have time to do this in prison, since there won't be any dogs there. Wait. I think there are therapy dogs or something. Maybe I can claim insanity and be entitled to a therapy dog.

Officer DeMarzo comes in and leads me into another room, furnished with a desk and two chairs. All the inspiration of the John Coltrane story fades to black when I see the torture device atop the desk: a telephone.

"Have a seat," he says. I sit in the discomfort of a plastic chair. Officer DeMarzo leans back against the edge of the desk, casually crossing one ankle over the other. This is probably not a good time to ask about Randy's flea allergy and whether the ointment Mom prescribed is working. He stares at me for a minute, and I swear, I feel pins pricking my skin.

"What is your phone number?" he asks.

There is nothing worse than what he is about to do.

I recite my number and he calls my mom.

"Dr. Kaplan?" He pauses. "This is Officer DeMarzo over at the police station. We have your daughter, Natalie, here." He pauses again; I think for dramatic effect. "No, she's not hurt, ma'am." Guilt. "We picked up your mother, too." He looks at me and listens. "Oh. Well, no, your mother is here by default, ma'am." Another pause. "Let me hand the phone over to Natalie so she can tell you why she's here."

Go ahead and just shoot me.

Numb. Tears form in my eyes, and everything I didn't do the past sixteen years suddenly contorts into everything I did do this week. Officer DeMarzo, still gripping the phone, holds it out to me.

I take the receiver and hold it on my lap for a second. I lift the phone, which feels like a twenty-pound weight, to my ear. "Mom?"

"What. Are. You. Doing. At. The. Police. Station?"

"I was trespassing."

"Where?"

"In a vacant house." John Coltrane could have told his mother he was practicing saxophone in a vacant house so he wouldn't disturb others, and that excuse probably would have flown. Me, I have no reason to be in a vacant house. This is now positively clear.

"Were you doing drugs?" The question reveals her biggest fear.

"No, Mom." I do not mention I was topless.

"Is Carver with you?" Her tone is rising.

More evidence against him. "Yes."

For a long time there is silence on the other end of the line. It sounds like a hole too deep to dig out of.

A dog's fear is often disguised as aggression.

—Michael Kaplan, *The Manifesto of Dog*

A half hour or an hour could've passed; I'm not sure. Fear obscures the passing of time. All I know is that I've been alone in this bare room for too long. After a while, I hear the muffled voices of a man and a woman talking, then the open yawn of the door. It's Mom.

Her eyes are red and swollen. She's unable to lift her feet; her clogs scuff against the floor. The hair pulled back in her clip is the only evidence of order. She sits in the chair behind the desk.

"What were you doing in that house?" she asks.

This is it. I can be scared or I can face this. "Carver and I were talking."

"The truth, Natalie. No more bullshit." Mom just said "bullshit."

"It is the truth. Would you rather I say we were downing shots of tequila?"

"Don't get smart with me." She is practically grinding her teeth.

"Truth? Carver was hiding in the back of the car tonight when I took Grandma to the senior center. I got scared and made him get out of the car. Then, after I dropped off Grandma, I felt like a coward. So I found Carver and we went into the house together."

"Why would you do that?" Mom asks, confused. "Why?"

And I think about it. I think about it enough that embers begin to kindle in my stomach, flames lick their way up to my throat, and I say it in my head until there's an inferno on the tip of my tongue. "Because normally, I wouldn't do that. Because being good has gotten me nowhere! You've never even told me that you're proud of me, that you're happy about the choices I've made. You just keep pointing out my imperfections. So I said screw it! Why not earn your disappointment instead?"

"Natalie." Mom stands up. "Do not yell at me."

I jump to my feet and meet her eye, keeping my voice raised. "If I don't yell, how else are you going to hear me!"

I sit back down in my chair, my body arching into a hump. "It's like whatever I say goes into this catcher's mitt of yours and gets thrown right back at me. It's like you keep expecting me to be this person that I'm not. I'm not you, Mom. And I realize I'm not who you want me to be, either. But can't you listen to me or even try to trust me?"

I look up at Mom through my tears. She sits down in her chair, stunned. Somehow, we've lost each other. This is a woman I used to want to impress; lately, I just want to piss her off.

"Mom, can you at least acknowledge that I have a brain? I may have lied this past week, but I also used my better judgment. I could easily have smoked pot, had sex, overdosed on wine—"

Mom raises her hand in protest. "Whoa, wait a minute—"

"No, Mom, you wait." Mom purses her lips, crosses her arms over her chest, and nods. "Up until now, you've been my compass. I hear your voice say no before mine has the opportunity to speak. I want to know what *I* sound like. You've got to stop suffocating me."

"Suffocate?" Mom asks, a pained look flashing across her face. "Do I really suffocate you?"

"That's what it feels like."

Mom stares at me, unflinching. I wonder if she's even breathing. Then she shows me a sign of life, uncrossing her arms. "Maybe I've made the mistake of making you think I am in charge of everything, including your life. I can own that. What I can't do, what

I won't do, is let you do whatever you want to do and have you expect me to approve."

"I've lived with you long enough to know that. I am not asking you to let me do anything I want." I pull a piece of flaked skin from my thumbnail and think for a minute about what I'm going to say before uttering another word. "Just give me an opportunity to find my boundaries before setting them for me. Like with Carver. Had I listened to you and kept it all professional, I'd never have gotten to know him or know that there's a side of me that is brave, that I can say no when I'm uncomfortable with something. Can you at least trust that?"

"I don't know," Mom says. "You haven't been honest with me."

"I can be honest with you, Mom. But you have to trust me, too. And maybe you can let me know that I'm okay once in a while. That I'm not just a source of frustration for you."

Mom slides out of her chair and kneels down in front of me, placing her hands on my knees. Looking at her, I see the signs of age that have sprouted in the last couple of years. Brushstrokes of thin lines frame her eyes; her skin has ripened like a soft peach. "I am proud of you, Natalie. Every time you walk into the clinic, my day is better because you're there. You are a sensitive, bright, and caring young woman. That's what I mean when I tell you I love you."

Sometimes we don't realize what we need to hear from someone else until they say it. There's a little shame in knowing I need my mother to tell me that I'm okay, that she's proud of me.

I'm human, though. I bet John Coltrane, as good as he was, needed the applause of an audience. Even dogs need some approval after they've retrieved a ball.

"So what about trusting me?" I ask.

"As much as I love you, I'm not going to walk out of this room with unabated trust in you. That is going to take time."

"Urgh!" I yell, grabbing my head. "Then what is the point of this whole conversation?"

Mom takes my hands in hers. "The point, Natalie, is that I hear you, okay? You need me to listen, and I am going to do my best to hear you."

It's not perfect, but it's a start, I guess.

"What will happen to Carver?" I ask as Mom and I walk out of the small room and into the stark hallway.

Mom stops us outside the door. "He needs to get his story straight. I spoke to him first and he said it was his idea to go into the house." He shouldered the blame? "If he plans to stay the rest of the summer, the three of us need to have a long talk."

"Mom, it was my fault, too."

"I'll trust you on that one."

*   *   *

Vernon had to give Mom a ride to the police station, since her car was parked on Juniper. When Mom and I walk into the lobby, Vernon, Grandma, and Carver are waiting.

Carver arches his eyebrows at me and I do the same, talking back in code but not sure of what we're saying. Grandma struggles out of her seat, waving Vernon away as he tries to help her.

The car ride home is still. Carver and I sit in the backseat, on either side of Mom. Grandma sits up front with Vernon. She, too, is quiet. Vernon drops me off at Juniper Street, where the car is parked across from the vacant house.

I drive home, following Vernon's car, tracing the back of Carver's head; his messy hair is the most distinct feature of his outline. And to think, just a few weeks ago I thought my biggest worry this summer would be pretending to sip strawberry wine from a plastic cup.

The fog thickens as I drive. The specks of stars go unseen behind the bullying clouds, but perhaps what is out of sight need not be out of mind.

At home, I idle near the curb, waiting for Vernon to drop off Mom, Grandma, and Carver, before I pull into the driveway. Mom and Carver get out from the backseat. Carver rushes over to open the passenger door for Grandma. Her hand lurches out of the car, waving him away. Her tiny patent leather foot touches ground, and Carver leans toward her with his kindness, cradling her elbow and helping her out of the car despite her protest.

The headlights of Vernon's car illuminate their walk to the door. Vernon backs his car out of the driveway and heads toward the clinic.

I steer into the driveway, turn off the ignition, and linger in the car.

Carver waits with Grandma as Mom opens the front door. Once it's open, I can see Mom bending down to receive the dogs, petting each one, giving Pip an extra rub on his ear. This is one of the rare moments when I can see myself in her. And I feel sad, because I've really done my best in my life to fill the good-hardworking-daughter role Mom has created for me. It's just that when I step out of that role to be with my friends or save a dog or, most recently, kiss Carver, I feel like I'm doing something wrong, like I have to lie to make it look right to Mom.

Mom allows the dogs outside, where they engage in their sniff-and-pee routine. Grandma is already inside the house, but Mom and Carver stand on the porch, exchanging words. Both of them keep looking at me inside the car. Is she asking him to go home?

Deep breath.

The dogs whiz about the yard, circling the trees, marking plots of grass, running back and forth to Mom and Carver for a rub on the head or a pat on the back.

Carver places his hands in his pockets, looks at me in the car, and starts walking up the steps to the room above the garage. I watch until he is inside, the lights flick on, and the door shuts.

Mom stands at the open front door. She calls the dogs into the house. And they follow, without question. Mom does not have to chase them or yell to make them submit. They just whip their bodies into motion and heed her call.

When the dogs are in the house, Mom shuts the door and walks to the car, waiting for me. It's my turn.

I step out and into my mother's arms. Being true to myself and being honest with Mom is a conflict of interest. I understand that. But I can't lie anymore or stifle myself when I'm scared to ask for what I need. And somewhere between knowing that and being held in my mother's arms, I feel closer to who I am and what I want.

The relationship between dog and man is a journey, not a destination.

—Michael Kaplan, *The Manifesto of Dog*

I wake up the next morning under a thin layer of covers, surprised that sleep stole wakefulness so quickly. I don't remember looking at the ceiling or counting dog breeds last night, only scraping my toe on Fu-Fu and collapsing onto my bed.

Pip has wrapped himself around my left foot, making it impossible for me to move it without pushing him off. I contort my body toward the clock so as not to rustle him. Noon! Saturday.

Last night seems distant, like a page from an old diary begging to be revisited and analyzed. I was someone I had never been last night. One minute I was in a vacant house with Carver; the next minute I was at the police station with my mom. It's sort of scary how time can be a magic trick, a chain of events appearing and disappearing with sleight of hand.

So it's Saturday. No school. Probably no work, either, since Mom didn't wake me up. Pip untangles himself the minute my big toe twitches. His one brown eye glares at me, but he'll get over it. I change into some shorts, put my phone in my pocket, brush my teeth, and gather the dogs for a walk. Downstairs is a note from Mom saying she'll see me tonight.

Mom may have let Carver sleep in, too. Maybe if Carver isn't working, either, he'll go for a walk with us. It'll be good to talk with him, especially before we have the "big" talk with Mom.

The dogs follow me outside and up the stairs to Carver's room. I knock softly. When there's no response, I give the door a sequence of knocks that range from "Are you sleeping?" to "Open the door or I'll beat it down." Otto sniffs the bottom of the doorjamb. I turn the doorknob to see if it gives.

It does.

When I was nine years old, I packed a day's worth of food and hid behind the latticework of our old backyard. It was a summer day, and in back of the lattice, between the rusted tricycle and the green spiral of the garden hose, was shade. I hid there with a stopwatch to time how long it took for someone to come looking for me. Mom clocked in at 4 minutes, 3.75 seconds—quick, considering I had packed enough supplies for the entire day.

Standing here at the doorway of Carver's room, I imagine him playing the same game. I wait for him to pop out and yell my time.

But Carver is not here.

There are no open duffel bags on the floor. No clothes scattered about. I check the closet to make sure he didn't shove everything into its tiny square, but he's not there saying, "Fooled ya!"

Loss should be followed by weightlessness, but it's not. All the missing parts—the spark I carry when I see Carver, his smile, the knowing who I am around him—are absent, yet I feel a weight pressing down on my chest.

I go to sit on the edge of the futon. Is he really gone?

On the wall there is only one picture from his collection remaining: the picture of the dragonfly. I reach over to peel it off and notice writing on the back. The squashed all-caps penmanship emboldens the message.

Natalie,
   I hope you don't think I've abandoned you.
My mom arranged for me to come home.
Seems like you need some time and space to
work things out with your mom.
   I thought about sneaking into your house
to say good-bye, but then I realized that it
would be wrong, because I would want to kiss

271

you. Maybe I'm weak, but I can't kiss you
good-bye. Only hello kisses for us, Natalie.
Next time we'll meet in my garden, the
moon-viewing one. I didn't tell you about the
dragonflies. Hold on to this one until then.

Love,
Carver

And there's his phone number.

Pixie collapses. He is gone.

I place the picture next to me on the futon,
dragonfly-side up, and let my head drop to my hands.
Crying. Loudly enough that Southpaw pokes her
warm, wet nose into the crisscross of fingers over my
face to lick my cheeks. Pip and Otto nuzzle in to do the
same. They listen while I heave and sob.

The dogs' ears perk at the sound of footsteps trailing up the stairs. Wait. He's coming back!

"I came home for lunch today," Mom says, walking
through the doorway. I slump in disappointment,
tears falling down to my legs. "He's really gone."

"I've noticed," I say, snuffling. "Did you ask his
mom to make him leave?"

"You think I'd do that?" Mom asks, looking
wounded.

"He wasn't an inconvenience," I say.

"I didn't ask that he leave." Mom lets out a deep
breath. "Faith called me at work just now to tell me
Carver left early this morning. He took a taxi to the

airport, and he's on his way back home. I'm here to see if you're okay." Mom sits down next to me on the futon. "Are you?"

"I'm not sure. I really like him." I pull my shirt up to my nose and wipe it. "Even without your permission."

Mom reaches over to place a strand of fading blue hair behind my ear. We sit there for a while, Mom holding me, the dogs curled at my feet with heads down.

I appreciate the quiet, the fact that Mom isn't drumming the "You're too young! You're better off without him! There's other fish in the sea!" speech into my head. It's enough for her to hold me, to let me be what I am at this moment: heartbroken.

Mom stays with me until my whimpering subsides. Then she stands up and hands me the golden key that Carver left behind. She kisses the top of my head, and I watch her with my parched eyes as she leaves and shuts the door behind her.

All the space I've ever wanted is in my hand and it feels empty. Not so empty that I can't fill it, but enough that it would be an opportune time for Kirby to shout, "Irony!"

Dangling above my head is the disco ball. I stand up, plug in the spotlight, flick the switch on the mirror-covered orb, and sit down on the ground with Pip, Otto, and Southpaw. Southpaw rests her brindled head on my lap, the ooze from her mouth moistening my leg. I rub the coarse hair on her ears and look up at the spinning disco ball.

Tassels of daylight sneak through the drawn shades, blotting out the shuffle of specks on the ceiling. Without the contrast of the light mingling with the dark, it's difficult to see what's there.

Dog drool may be a breeding ground for invisible rabies germs, toilet tanks may be hiding places for bags of pot, and feelings may be pretended into near nonexistence. Just because something's hidden or even shadowed by something else doesn't mean it's not there. Knowing this, I pull my phone from my pocket.

I dial Carver's number. Pixie diligently rubs her own Foo dog with each ring. Then she starts to sashay around the arena of my heart when I hear his voice answer at the other end.

Acknowledgments

Dogs thrive in packs. So do I. Thanks to the following for their support in the breeding of this book.

THE GUIDE DOGS: Kim Douillard, Kathleen Gallagher, Danan McNamara, and Cheryl Ritter for inspiring me to write. Your solid encouragement and affirmation led me toward a novel.

THE HERDERS: Maria Bertrand, Beth Wagner Brust, Jayne Haines, Sarah Hansen, Jenny Moore, and John Ritter for the honest feedback and literary companionship. Without your active nudging and inspiration, I'd be grazing aimlessly in the wrong pasture.

THE GROOMERS: Mom, Dad, Mindy, and Eve for letting "book talk" enter our telephone conversations.

Melissa Taylor for her TLC of my children while I wrote. Ellen and Benny for unmitigated joy and laughter. And the hundreds of students I've had the honor of teaching: your voices continue to resonate.

THE GURUS: Sandy and Harry Choron; Stanley Coren; Dr. Nicholas Dodman; William Wegman, whose books gave me a deeper understanding of dogs; *The Bark* magazine, and the staff and dogs of the HSUS.

THE BREEDERS: Happy, grateful, yippy barks to my agent, Steven Chudney, for his efficiency and his belief in me; to the SCBWI for their life-changing organization; for the support of Beverly Horowitz, the fine-tuning of Jennifer Black and the production efforts of the team at Delacorte Press; and enormous gratitude to my editor, Claudia Gabel, who overlooked her allergy to dogs and gave me the opportunity to revisit my story under her tutelage.

THE GREAT STUD DOG: Mostly, thanks to my husband, Jeremy, who has given me his unconditional love, honesty, and precious room to write.

About the Author

When Stacey Goldblatt was in high school, she spent every Saturday at a family friend's veterinary clinic. Currently, she boards in San Diego with her husband, their two children, dog, and cat. This is her first novel. You can visit Stacey at www.staceygoldblatt.com.

the
everything store

JEFF BEZOS
AND THE AGE
OF AMAZON

BRAD STONE

Little, Brown and Company

New York   Boston   London

Little, Brown and Company
Hachette Book Group
237 Park Avenue, New York, NY 10017
littlebrown.com

First Edition: October 2013

Little, Brown and Company is a division of Hachette Book Group, Inc. The Little, Brown name and logo are trademarks of Hachette Book Group, Inc.

The publisher is not responsible for websites (or their content) that are not owned by the publisher.

The Hachette Speakers Bureau provides a wide range of authors for speaking events. To find out more, go to hachettespeakersbureau.com or call (866) 376-6591.

ISBN 978-0-316-21926-6 (hc) / 978-0-316-23990-5 (large print) / 978-0-316-25179-2 (international)
Library of Congress Control Number 2013941813

10 9 8 7 6 5 4 3 2 1

RRD-C

Printed in the United States of America

For Isabella and Calista Stone

When you are eighty years old, and in a quiet moment of reflection narrating for only yourself the most personal version of your life story, the telling that will be most compact and meaningful will be the series of choices you have made. In the end, we are our choices.

—Jeff Bezos, commencement speech at
Princeton University, May 30, 2010

Contents